A Window to Young Minds

Short Stories by Young Writers

Book One

Lune Spark

Lune Spark Books, Morrisville, NC

Publisher: Lune Spark LLC

PO Box 1443, Morrisville, NC, 27560, United States

www.lunespark.com

Young Writers' Resources: www.lunespark.com/youngwriters

E-mail: books@lunespark.com

Phone: +1 (919) 809-4235

Ordering Information: Quantity sales. Special discounts are available on quantity purchases by corporations, associations, and others. For details, contact the publisher at the address above.

Or visit www.lunespark.com.

ISBN 13: 978-1-947960-00-8

ISBN 10: 1-947960-00-8

Library of Congress Control Number: 2017916566
Lune Spark Books, Morrisville, NC

Cover art by Gauri Mishra

Digital art by Sakimi Chan

1. Short Stories 2. Anthology 3. Creative writing 4. Young writers

First edition

To the young writers whose storytelling talent is yet to be discovered. May the world find you soon!

Contents

Introduction

Our future depends on stories. As the world advances, literature has the ability to ground us—in our humanness, our imaginations, and our enlightenment. Fueled by the need to interpret the past, to explore the present, and to imagine the future, each generation shapes the world of books. In order to preserve this, we must have a new generation willing to share their stories. The support young writers receive is vital to whether they keep writing, and it fuels the stories yet to come.

However, this support does not always exist. Growing up in Aligarh, India, I had limited resources for sharing my writing. There was no platform for me to receive feedback or advice, and I struggled to find sincere reviewers. I kept writing, but many children do not. This problem drove me to where I am today. With the vision of supporting young writers, I started the annual *Lune Spark Short Story Contest* in May 2017. It is open to writers between the ages of ten and sixteen.

A Window to Young Minds is the first of the contest's yearly anthologies, *Short Stories by Young Writers*. The twenty-three wonderful stories in this book are handpicked from 2017's entries. The talent of these young writers shines in their command of storytelling and their unique take on genre—from telling a pirate love story to re-creating the Hindenburg disaster that happened on May 6, 1937, in New Jersey.

If the future depends on stories, then our future looks bright indeed.

I hope you like this anthology. These talented young writers would love to receive any feedback on their stories—leaving a review on a website or blog of your choice would help them in honing their skills further.

My special gratitude goes to the following individuals. Running the contest and publishing this book couldn't have been possible without your help!

- The participants of the 2017 *Lune Spark Short Story Writing* contest and their parents for all the enthusiasm and support.
- The judges of the 2017 contest: Anne Anthony, Monica Sanchez, Neal Katz, Owen Thomas, Russel Lazega, Ruth Moose, and Samantha Bryant. Thanks for your passion for this cause.
- The amazing volunteers for the contest: Krishna Rao, Melwyn Joachim, Neeraj Badaya, Prafull Porwal, Rhea Gonsalves, and Ritu Mishra. Your tremendous support made it possible to plan for and successfully execute such an ambitious project.

Pawan Mishra
Morrisville, NC
October 2017

The Skyfarer's Daughter

Cate Pitterle

(Age: Fifteen)

*T*he clouds are thick today. I can barely make out the ocean far below us as our ship plunges through the sky, its sails snapping in the wind. A faint dew covers the deck, and I scamper across it, my boots squealing. *No fear.* Not when a burly crewman bumps into me and swears, and not when I crash into the guardrail as the boat jars. Not even when the floating islands of Britain appear on the horizon, dark and sinister.

Using the guardrail to support me, I climb to the ship's bow. A cluster of boatmen sprawls on the open deck, swigging alcohol from stolen canisters. No one looks up as I approach. *Good.*

I sit down on the fringes of the group and strain to hear the conversation.

"Raid off Britain," says an older man. "Captain says it's good loot."

"Hah!" says another, sputtering in his drink. "Remember last raid? Fat lot that did for us."

There are mutters of agreement, and I find myself nodding. The last raid found our ship ruined by a British sloop and our crew short two men. They went overboard after a shell plunged into the hull. *Disastrous*, my father called it. Our ship almost fell from the sky, and it took no shortage of men to keep the hull airtight.

Suddenly the group's conversation stalls. I look up just as the men scramble to their feet, their gazes fixated on the figure striding toward us. *The captain.* He wears his black coat today, and it's crusted with blood from the last raid. I tear my eyes away, not bothering to stand. He reaches us and glares at me, his eyes smoldering like cinders.

"Janis."

He doesn't bother saying anything else. I stand as he marches toward me. When he reaches me, he grips my arm and not gently. I grit my teeth to keep from whimpering.

"Hello, Father," I mutter. He doesn't respond.

He turns and drags me away from the crew, across the swaying deck. No one questions him. No one ever questions my father.

Except me.

The ship's stern is raised, leaving space for a small room built into it. Father drags me to it, thrusts open the door, and pushes me inside. He lets the head wind slam the door shut behind us.

"This needs to stop," he says as he sits down at his desk—well, at the shipping crate that serves as one. He was rich once, but he turned to pirating after my mother left.

Anger sparks through me as I look at him, and I see it in him, too—a fire ignited in his eyes.

"Janis," he says. "You must end this…friendship with that boy. He is not worth your time, yet all the crew is talking about it."

A laugh bubbles in my throat, and I bite my lip to keep it from escaping. *Of all things to chide me for.* Heaven forbid Edward Gull, terror of the skies, would allow his daughter to love a lowly boatman.

"You're kidding," I say. "He's smart and funny, and he loves me, which is more than I can say for *some* of the crew."

Father scoffs. "You have standards, Janis. There are fifty men on this ship, and you choose the scrawny orphan?"

"And your standards are so high," I say. "Having an illegitimate daughter is much more socially acceptable."

He starts, shock creeping onto his face. It's gone in an instant. "You ungrateful child," he snarls, slowly rising from his chair. "You are a disgrace to your mother's name."

He slams a fist down on the crate, and it bangs from the impact. I cringe, dread pooling in my stomach.

He raises a hand, and I wince, waiting for the pain. It never comes. Instead, Father points to the door.

"Get out," he growls.

I stand and stumble from the room, pushing into open air. The scent of rain hits me, along with a soft fog. *We're in a cloud.* I scramble through the haze, willing my heart to stop thundering.

I walk along the rigging until I feel a solid, worn pole: the crow's nest. I smile as I reach for the net beside it, my fingers curling around the rough rope. I hoist myself up just as the ship bursts through the fog, revealing a sunlit sky all the way to Britain's outline. The ocean shimmers far below, pale gold wherever the sun's rays hit.

I settle back against the nest's wooden bars. My shoulders slump, and I relax the second before I feel the brush of a hand on my arm.

I whirl around and frown as I see autumn-red hair and startled blue eyes. The boy meets my bewildered gaze and breaks into a grin, laughing as I pull him into a hug. I sigh.

"Tiernan, thank heavens. I thought you were amidships."

"Wouldn't miss this for the world," he says. "You're late."

A Window to Young Minds

"Got pulled into my father's office. He was furious."

His eyes glint with curiosity. "What about?"

"Nothing," I say quickly. "Just about staying away from that new guy, James."

A frown tugs at Tiernan's lips. "You haven't gone near him since he came on, Janis." He pauses. "It was about me, wasn't it?"

My silence is answer enough, and he sighs, wrapping his arms around me. My stomach flips, and I curl around to gaze at him.

"I wish we could do this every day."

"We barely get to talk." Smirking, he bends down and kisses me. "For lost time."

I smile back, holding his light gaze in mine. Then letting his arms fall away, I stand and start to climb down the net.

"What are you doing?" he asks, his eyebrows knitting together.

I grin. "Haven't you heard? We're going on a raid."

That's when the boat's horn wails.

I clap my free hand to my ear, my heart racing. Blood roars through me, and I gasp with the shock of adrenaline. I force myself to grab the net with both hands and continue descending. Tiernan follows, quick and surefooted.

We reach the deck in seconds. The crew is everywhere, and the sound of clanging swords fills my ears like a heartbeat. A great boom follows. The cannons. They're firing.

All at once I sight the enemy ship: a huge man-o'-war flying a brightly colored flag. The flag of Britain.

The Brits glide closer until the side of their ship smacks into ours. The deck shudders, and I stumble as I try to keep my footing.

"Tiernan," I yelp, but the wind rips my words away as the British crew jumps, one by one, onto our ship.

A cannonball flies over my head, and Tiernan forces me down as it crashes onto the deck behind us.

"Go," he gasps. "Get to the office, somewhere. Run!"

Terror shoots through me, sharp and raw. I slide a dagger from my boot, but we both know I can't use it. I've never fought a day in my life.

As Tiernan draws his sword, I run. Every step makes me feel like a coward. My feet are lead dragging behind me. *I can't make it.* The thought is a certainty, thrumming like a second heartbeat. *I can't make it.*

A pile of barrels rests against the rigging beside me. I hear a crash from behind—*a Brit*—and I dive between a crack in two barrels and scramble for cover. I crouch down, my breathing ragged, hot fear tearing through my veins. The crack yawns before me, giving an ample view of the fight. Swords whirl between sweaty men, a deadly display of silver and brawn. My gaze snaps toward the fringes of the fight where a black-coated man struggles against a privateer twice his size.

My heart stops. *Father.*

He stumbles, his foot catching on a curved plank. He's injured. That must be why he's losing. *Father never loses.* The Brit slices his sword, and Father barely catches it. On the next swing, he falls.

As the privateer raises his sword, I close my eyes, expecting Father to scream.

He doesn't.

My eyes fly open to see Tiernan standing over my father, leveling his sword at the privateer. Father lifts his head, shocked. Tiernan slices at the privateer, and a red spray flies through the air.

Then a whistle blows from the British ship, and the privateer's face dissolves into terror. He looks over his shoulder, and the sword falls from his hand, forgotten. I don't hear the clang as it hits the deck. I can barely think.

The privateer doesn't look back as he rushes to his ship. Around us, the other privateers do the same; their crew is decimated, almost gone. Blood covers our deck like a carpet. The privateers leap back to their ship, over thousands of feet of sky and ocean. In the chaos, some of their men plunge into open air.

And there is Tiernan extending a hand for my father to take.

Tiernan saved him. He saved my blasted father.

I barely feel my feet as I scramble up and dash to Tiernan. He falls into my outstretched arms, and I take in his warm, sweaty scent. He grins and whispers words I don't hear. So I watch his lips instead.

"I love you," he says. "I love you."

I smile. Even my father can't change that.

An Unexpected Journey

Charlotte Menke

(Age: Fourteen)

I dragged my worn leather boots along the dusty concrete slabs of the loading dock. As I maneuvered through the sea of people, I picked up bits of German farewells. The blimp dock in Frankfurt buzzed with excitement.

I tightened my grip on the worn handle of my suitcase and frowned at the flapping swastikas on flags that danced in the breeze. They taunted my faith, and I loathed their presence.

A snap of my lederhosen suspender made me jump. I turned around to find my younger brother, Hans, with a glimmer in his eyes.

"Peter!" Hans cried. "Look at the big balloon!"

I couldn't scold him. Not today. Not when I felt his excitement, too. I smiled at the huge blimp that towered high above. Then I swooped my giggling brother onto my shoulders so that he could have a better view at the magnificent airship.

"Hindenburg, that's what they call it," I exclaimed. "The fastest blimp of the century, and we're gonna ride it!"

Hans wiggled off me and then tightened his grip on his ragged teddy bear. We leaped up each step that led to the entrance of the blimp.

"What do you think you're doing?"

A scowling man with a long white beard blocked our path

at the top. His uniform told me he must be the captain. My hand shook terribly as I held out the tickets that would send us to America.

"Sir." I gulped, trying to mask the fear in my voice, waiting as he checked our tickets. Nervous thoughts flooded my mind—*what if there was a mistake and we wouldn't be granted access?* "I'm a mighty fine worker. I'd be glad to be put to work. I need any scrap of money I can get my hands on to send to my mother while I'm gone."

"Let me see these hands of yours." The captain ran his fingers over my blisters. "Large, strong hands ya got, son. Fine hands for a dishwasher."

He slapped me on the back before sending me to the kitchen. I gave Hans's little hand a gentle squeeze. Mama would make it the end of me if I lost him.

We reached the kitchen quickly, eagerness in our every step.

"Hey!" a tall boy about my age hollered, waving around a wet mop in the air. He wore a white, button-down, flannel shirt and suspenders similar to my own. He ran his fingers through his dirty-blond hair, revealing daring blue eyes.

"Look what you did, tracking dirt right across the floor I just cleaned!"

I whipped my head around, studied my recent path, and was puzzled to see not a bit of mud.

"Aw, got ya there. Kidding." He playfully punched my shoulder. "Werner Franz," he said.

I exhaled. Before I could reply, Werner whisked me out of the lobby for a tour of the blimp, his mouth never ceasing to quiet.

"And this is our cabin!" Werner exclaimed. The blimp was

Short Stories by Young Writers

rising, and I watched through the window how each handcrafted roof of Frankfurt grew smaller.

"Ya sure don't talk a lot. Hey, what's your name anyway?" Werner said.

I laughed. How was I to get any words out around him?

"I'm Peter Kolisch. I'm heading to America to escape Hitler's reign."

"This is my ticket out, too. Working on the Hindenburg beats living on the streets," he said.

A pit of homesickness formed in my stomach. How I longed for my rusty blue bike and the crisp air of Germany. The image of my mama, her eyes swollen with tears, popped into my head. I wished she could have come with us to America, away from the brewing danger.

"My mother takes care of my sick grandparents," Peter said. "My father died a war hero."

Werner shot me a sad smile and slung an arm over my shoulder.

Suddenly Hans appeared in the doorway, one hand on his teddy and the other interlocked with the captain. His grinning face was smeared with chocolate.

"Peter, this is Capin' Heinrich! He showed me the engine and gave me these!" Hans held out a handful of Beachee nut chocolate drops, a luxury.

"Hans!" I grabbed him and gave him a tight squeeze.

Captain Heinrich grinned and explained that Hans had been a delight, entertaining the other officers.

I felt a rush of relief. "Thank you, Captain."

"Good night, boys. Sleep well."

Early the next morning, I woke to the sound of Hans crying.

"What is it little one?" I rubbed his back, trying to comfort him.

"I miss my Ima. When is she comin' to America?"

At that moment I realized how hard our separation would be on him. Mama had told me to keep Hans safe and live a better life with our uncle. Would we ever see her again? My eyes welled with tears.

"I'm not sure, Hans. It'll be OK."

Hans rubbed the back of his hand under his nose and sniffled.

"Come on, boys! It's us three now!" Werner leaped from the bunk and dragged us out of bed. "Dishwasher duty."

In the kitchen, I moaned at the stack of dirty dishes. Werner picked up Hans and set him on the counter, a towel in his hand. "We'll all help," Werner said.

Together we tossed soapsuds in the air and smacked each other with wet towels. Our new friendship reassured me that not all happiness would be lost.

Suddenly the Hindenburg began to tilt.

"Whoa." Werner grabbed onto a cabinet handle to steady himself. Terror filled his eyes, and Hans let out a cry.

I panicked, frozen still. Werner's once lively face was still like a statue.

Dishes fell from the cabinet and shattered on the floor.

An explosion sounded.

My body leaped into action. I grabbed Hans off the counter and ran into the keel walkway, with Werner at my heels. To my horror, a giant fireball was blazing toward us.

Smoke flooded the halls, and ashes caught in my throat. As the ship tilted farther, we slid toward the flames and away from the bow.

Instinctively I grabbed for the ropes that lined the side of the hall and lifted Hans away from the inferno. I hung on, my blisters bursting open, as the ship jarred.

We were seconds away from landing. Through the window, I saw the people at the naval air station in Lakehurst, New Jersey, screaming and running at the sight of the Hindenburg, instead of waving and taking pictures. I spotted a water ballast tank alongside the walkway, farther down the hall. I pulled it off its mounting and soaked Hans, Werner, and myself. It would be our shield against the swallowing flames. Werner snapped to his senses, and the three of us tightened our grips on the wet ropes.

We needed a way out.

My vision was blurred from flying flurries, but I spotted a hatch in the back of the kitchen that would be our only escape. Werner helped me force the hatch open as the airship plummeted. It was now or never.

I threw Hans out the hatch and watched him fall toward the ground. Next it was me or Werner. I shoved my beloved friend away from the fire and toward the American soil.

"Peter!" Werner bellowed, falling.

"Go!" My scream came from deep in my heart. Fire and chunks of the Hindenburg shot out around me. I was launched into the air.

My eyes slowly opened as I regained consciousness. Hans and my uncle Bernard were huddled around me. I pulled off my once-white, button-down shirt, which was now scorched from the flames. My body was covered in burns that would eventually heal, but they would leave a scar on me forever.

"Peter, you are my hero." Hans sniffled and crawled closer. He rubbed my back, the way I always did to him.

A Window to Young Minds

Bodies covered the ground, and the sky was gray with grief.

Werner appeared amid the scene of death, holding Hans's teddy bear.

"He survived, too." Werner handed the bear to Hans. He slung an arm over my shoulder and said, "You really are my best friend. You saved my life. I'm sure your dad would be mighty proud."

His words swelled in my chest. My father died a hero, and maybe I was a hero as well.

"Where's Capin'?" Hans asked, looking around for his good friend.

Werner's sad smile turned into a devastating frown, and his eyes filled with despair. He said, "Captain Heinrich is in a better place now."

Hans squeezed my hand hard at the news and held back his emotion. It bothered me how in such a short period of time Hans had taught himself to do this. We started to make our way to the car, arms around each other. Staying strong together.

My uncle pushed a curl of dark hair out of my face. "Peter, Hans, Werner, look at this soil. It is American," he said in his thick German accent. "Hold it."

"It looks just like the soil in Germany," Hans said, staring at the handful he cradled.

"No, child. This soil is a chance at a new life. Put Germany behind you, my boys. Thrive."

My uncle pointed at a small dandelion that stood tall amid the wreckage.

"Like that hopeful little flower, grow, even when the world around you is burning."

Spoilers of the Future

Sreya Vannapagari

(Age: Thirteen)

"You're only seventeen. There'll be time to settle down later! Right now you need to be out, meeting people, going on dates!" Alex pestered, chasing me down our school's hallway.

This was the fourth time that week he was bothering me about dating. He went through girlfriends like a sick kid went through tissues and was peeved that I had no interest in getting a girlfriend.

I brushed past a girl whose arms were laden with binders and books. My elbow made contact with her shoulder. I flinched away, but it was too late. I saw visions of this girl clinging onto my arm, with me trying to shake her off. There were dates that ended with her screaming at me and dinners that amounted into a tantrum. It all ended with her dumping lemonade over my head.

These visions were what I liked to call my *insurance*. Whenever I touched someone for the first time, I saw the future I shared with that person, all in just a moment. It was a power I had possessed ever since I could remember. I hadn't realized it was abnormal until I was seven, when I had mentioned it to my mom, who looked at me like I had grown another head. Ever since, I had kept my power secret. I had read too many stories about "freaks" who were experimented on, and I didn't want a life like that. However, it was a useful thing to have. I knew exactly how all my relationships would

A Window to Young Minds

work out.

Although, of course, it could get annoying sometimes. The visions lasted only moments, but they always startled me. I had quit every team sport I tried due to the inconvenience of having visions every time I made contact with someone. Every crush I'd ever had ended with a bad vision. Most of them were just texts that never got replies or avoidance in school. Some had more malicious endings, and although I was glad to avoid such a situation, I wanted to go through things like heartbreak without knowing exactly how things would end. It was like I was being spoiled for every single book I started reading. What was the point in continuing if I knew what the result would be?

"Leave me alone, Alex. I've told you. I haven't got any interest in dating," I muttered.

"What about that girl back there? The brunette?" He gestured to the girl I had just brushed against, the one who, if we were to date, would end up dumping a drink over my head.

"No way," I responded. "Would you just let it go? We're not all interested in girls."

Alex raised an eyebrow and smirked.

"Ah, OK. You shoot for the other team? How about him then?" he asked, pointing to a sophomore with pale blond hair and a smattering of freckles that nearly blended in with his tanned skin.

"I'm not going to say he isn't attractive, because you don't need to be gay to appreciate someone's good looks, but I'm not gay! I just don't want to date. What's the big deal?" I demanded.

Alex threw his hands up in surrender.

"I was just trying to help," Alex said, feigning hurt. I elbowed him in the ribs.

"Drop it, OK? I'll date whenever I feel like it," I responded, shaking my head.

"Fine," he grumbled, with a pout that spoke volumes about his annoyance.

"Thank you," I responded. "Now go to class. You're supposed to be across the school."

It dawned on him that I was right.

"See you later!" he called, running off.

I chuckled, shaking my head. As I walked into my classroom, a tall Asian girl bumped into me. I cringed and waited to see something awful, but what I saw was different.

I saw a first date at the roller-skating rink ending in us falling over laughing. More dates like this flashed by, with us sharing food and smiles, and then it progressed to stolen kisses or texting for hours at a time. Yet there was still more good to come. I saw us together through college and then a casual wedding set in a meadow. Pink flowers were threaded through her dark hair. There were kids, smiles, all-around happiness. I had never seen something like this before.

When the visions ended, I was in absolute awe of what I had seen. I had never met someone who would have a long-term relationship with me.

The girl mumbled a quick sorry and walked off before I had a chance to say anything. I looked back at her figure receding down the hallway, my eyes wide.

"Are you going to go, or..." A kid behind me looked at me strangely.

"Oh, yeah, sorry," I said quickly, hurrying into the room. Still fixated on that girl, I sat down at my desk. I hadn't ever

A Window to Young Minds

given her more than a moment's thought before now. Though I had seen her around, I only knew her name: Janie. I had no connection to her whatsoever, but things were different now.

I have to do something about her, I thought. The bell interrupted my thoughts, startling me.

The whole day was filled with thoughts of Janie and of things I could do. She was in two of my classes, English and band. Band didn't really count, as she was a flute and I was a tenor saxophone, meaning we sat on different sides of the room, but English was a possibility.

And so my mission began.

It took nearly two months to build what I hoped was a friendship with Janie. She didn't talk much, but she was pretty funny when you listened to what she had to say. She mumbled little quips under her breath during English that always made me smile. Throughout this time, I kept my goal in mind, but it was great getting to know Janie regardless. She was different than what I had expected, probably because I didn't know her at all. I had written her off as someone uninteresting, but like people always said, you can't judge a book by its cover.

It was slow going at first. It wasn't easy to work up the courage to start talking to her, much less ask her out, even if I *knew* what would happen. My powers had never failed me before, but what if, in the most crucial moment, they did?

Yet in late March, I finally did it. I mustered up the courage to ask her out. It wasn't going to be easy, especially doing it for the first time, but in some ways, I was excited. I've always been someone who just wanted to settle down. I wasn't like Alex, who liked dating, although, to be fair, he didn't have any idea what his future with those girls would be.

Short Stories by Young Writers

At least not in the definite way I did.

"Janie?" I asked. "Can I talk to you?"

Janie's binder had exploded, so she was gathering her papers. I bent down and helped her collect them all.

"How cliché," I muttered.

"What?" she asked, shoving a pile of papers into a folder.

"I don't think this is the best time to ask you, but..." I paused for a moment, a sudden bout of unsureness washing over me.

"But what?" Janie demanded.

"Uh...do you wanna...go out sometime?" I asked awkwardly, stumbling over the simple sentence.

"No!" Janie shrieked.

My stomach dropped.

"Oh, o—"

"No, that's not what I meant," Janie laughed. "I was going to ask you today, too!"

"Oh!" I said, surprised.

"Just text me later. I gotta go now," she said, grabbing the rest of her belongings. I stared after her, my stomach still fluttering.

I had never thought my powers could be something I could use to influence my life so much, regardless of whether it was in a negative or positive way. Sure, I avoided pointless dates or friendships with people who would end up drifting away, but I hadn't experienced something like this, something so sure. Our first date was magical, but so was every other moment we spent together.

Yet all I could think throughout our time together was, *What if I was wrong?* But as our relationship stayed concrete over the years, my doubts dissolved. I wasn't wrong, and for

A Window to Young Minds

once, I was glad. Maybe my power was annoying sometimes, but I wouldn't trade it for the world. Nothing else could have led me to Janie the way it did, and I knew I owed it a lot.

Short Stories by Young Writers

Wynter

Ayanna Schubert

(Age: Fourteen)

The snow fell softly around the child's feet, and the whispers grew louder with each step forward. The child glanced around, eagerly staring out into the dark forested boundary of her home. She had been waiting for hours but wasn't quite ready to give up on him. He had said he would be back today, and by God, he'd better be back.

She could only imagine what their reunion would be like. He would lumber out of the forest, his sword falling at his side when he saw her. He would smile, and she would cry. She'd run up to him in the deep snow, tears streaming off her pale face. He would hug her so tight that she would think that he was trying to strangle her. She would try to wrap her tiny arms around him and would be barely able to get her arms around half of his waist. It would be a beautiful meeting. A silent reunion of souls in the night.

She couldn't stand the wait; she had to see him now. She bounced up and down on her little feet. But then she had a thought. A dark thought.

She had heard around town that this year the wolves were becoming more aggressive, what with them going hungry because of the long period of snow so early in the fall season. She stopped smiling and stood at a standstill. She thought of the bodies that had surfaced, brutally torn to shreds. She felt a familiar feeling in her stomach. She turned around

A Window to Young Minds

nervously and listened for the howls of passing wolves.

Not a sound.

She let out a breath she had been holding in and sank to the ground, snow burying her legs. She had imagined the worst and was currently picturing his mutilated corpse mangled, dripping tiny red droplets onto the freshly fallen snow. A lump grew in her throat.

Surely he's strong enough to fight any wolf, she thought, trying to look on the bright side. Of course her mind went back to the thought of the wolves ganging up on him, lunging forward, sinking fangs into soft flesh. She let out a soft whimper.

The night swallowed the noise that escaped her throat. The wind had begun to pick up and whipped her face with its ice-cold tendrils. No longer was the thought of him keeping her warm. She now began to think about how she was all alone. There wasn't another soul for miles. She was truly alone. He wasn't coming back. He had never planned to.

That explained the abundant supplies that had disappeared and the way he had left without saying good-bye. She had pondered this, trying to make excuses for him that he was in a hurry or that he had, in fact, kissed her forehead before he left.

But it was true what they said. He was gone. She was alone. She had no one. She would die without him. She had never learned how to fend for herself. He had always said she was too young and fragile. And now it was too late.

Her legs began to shake—of the cold or her impending death, she wasn't sure.

She listened to the whispers that had begun up again. "He's gone," they told her. She felt an unnatural feeling of calmness and acceptance. She looked up the black sky. The moon hung over her, staring back. Smiling, she listened to the whispers once more and leaned back in the snow. She was positive he had died a long time ago.

The note on her bedside table had done nothing to confirm her suspicions. *Out hunting. Back in a few days*, it had read. She came to the conclusion that he had left her. At least that's what they had said, sending her looks between whispers. She had looked at him for guidance, but he was looking straight ahead, stoic.

She remembered one of them saying that they were running out of money, that he was going to leave her for someone much older. Someone who could take care of things. She had been a burden that he never asked for. She wanted to believe it was all gossip, but it looked like they were right. Of course they were. Being a child, she didn't understand the world, or that's what everyone said.

Now she was paying for it. Not that she could do anything about it in the first place.

The snow wrapped around her, swallowing her whole. It had been snowing for days, accumulating until it had reached a few feet, the highest it had been in decades. The snow had brought silence with it, for a time. Then the voices had started again. A smile played at her face as she remembered how he had always told her to ignore them. But she found it difficult to ignore something that had made its home in her head.

Still smiling, she let the snow seep into her clothes, making her shiver uncontrollably. She laughed at the thought of him watching this unfold. Something in the back of her mind almost *wanted* him to be somewhere out there watching her.

The snow still fell, melting when it touched her skin. She frowned when she realized that it would take forever to die

A Window to Young Minds

like this. Sure, the cold would get her sooner or later. But this was much too tedious.

She tried to get up but found that her muscles would not move. She was stuck there. She huffed, annoyed at the fact that she was now stuck being bored to death. Quite literally.

It was only a few minutes later that she began to grow completely calm. Her body felt numb, and she no longer cared about what was going to happen to her. She couldn't differentiate the cold from the warmth. Her brain was no longer functioning properly, and she quickly slipped into a catatonic state.

Hours later he found her, frozen and blue. He lifted her into his arms, cradled her head, and kissed her forehead. He brought her inside although he knew it was much too late for her. Yet his face remained blank and expressionless.

That night she died in his arms.

Hesitating at first, he glanced over her body, thin and weak. He had spent so long in the brutal cold, shivering as he had hunted for food, unable to find anything. The pangs had become so painful.

That spring when the snow began to recede into the earth, he brought out her bones, grief and guilt heavy on his shoulders, and laid her to rest in a shallow grave under an old oak tree.

Short Stories by Young Writers

The King of the Board

Sonia Birla

(Age: Thirteen)

Allan's alarm clocks could be described as a cross between a guttural cry and a howling wolf. He had five. They were a revolting thing to wake up to every morning.

This morning was different. Allan didn't wake up ready to destroy every person involved in the creation of these horrid contraptions. When Allan sat up in his bed, he was greeted with the smell of pancakes wafting in the air and stacks of old, dusty cassettes littering the floor.

Allan sat up and rubbed his eyes a few times to make sure he was awake. After the momentary realization that food was available, Allan not so gracefully jumped out of his bed and tripped down the stairs, landing in a heap at the bottom. He groaned and blinked his eyes. Allan gasped when he saw who was looking down at him.

"Grandpa?" Allan asked incredulously. "Y-you're here?"

"I live here. What are you talking about, son?" He smiled brightly and set down a stack of pancakes on the table. "Eat up! You need the energy to prepare for that competition!"

For the next few minutes, the pancakes didn't matter; the grandfather did. Allan ran back up the stairs into his room. He needed confirmation. His bare walls had been replaced with images of champion chess players, and his bookshelf was lined with books on chess theory. He spun on his heels to the giant glass case beside the door. It was full of golden trophies glistening in the morning sun that was streaming through the window.

Allan fell back onto his bed. Even the ceiling was exactly the same as it had been. Allan could still see the dents of when he had gotten so fed up with losing that he had thrown his glass pieces at the ceiling, shattering them.

It all hit him at once. Allan opened his mouth to scream. Tears welled up in his eyes. He began shaking uncontrollably. Every thought he had had after that day played in his mind as if someone had used a universal remote to play it in a loop in his head. The voices got louder.

"Did you hear? His grandfather died."

"OMG, he plays chess? That's so lame!"

"What's wrong with you?"

The voices got louder. They got louder. They got even louder.

And then there was nothing.

The tears in his eyes disappeared. The scream aching to fly out of his lips was muted. The voices in his head were silenced. There was nothing but the faint chirping of cicadas outside his window.

"Oh, God. Those time demons got to you already, huh? Pesky little guys."

The voice seemed to be echoing from every direction.

"Who was that?" Allan said as he flew up from his sleeping position with his scrawny arms pulled into fists. He was met with a man with a top hat and a cane. A light stubble rested on his cheeks, and a French mustache adorned his face.

"Me? I don't matter." The man looked like he was trying hard to put on a jolly visage. "I'm here as a messenger of sorts from the gods. Long story short, they thought your life was pitiful. And the cause for it was the events of tomorrow, the whole Grandpa-dying, losing-chess-competition thing and so on. So they gave you a chance to fix things. Tomorrow night you will be sent back to your time. Anything you change here will have an effect on your future."

He paused for a second. "I think that's all they wanted me to tell you. Adios!"

"Wait!" Allan called.

"What?" the man asked, annoyance lacing his voice. "I am on a schedule, you know. The next year I have to go is 1215. And then to 9567. I don't have time for this!"

"Why me?"

"That's a stupid question. I'm leaving."

"No! Wait, please!"

"Ugh. You were supposed to do great things. And you didn't. It's a matter of failed expectations. I'm going now!"

That stung. "What great things?"

"I dunno! Do you *think* they tell the messengers everything? *No.* They don't. Good-bye."

Despite Allan's calls, the man didn't come back. Allan was dumbfounded. Gods, as in plural, existed. And they cared about what he did. It was a lot to process. Luckily he didn't have time to. His feet carried him down the stairs, against the will of his brain.

Allan thought he could handle talking to his grandfather, "Good morning." He nodded when he reached the last step, but faltered when his foot touched the hardwood, "I'm going to practice for tomorrow!"

"Wait, Allan!" his grandfather called from down the stairs. Allan paused halfway up, not daring to look down at his face.

"Are you OK? You seemed kind of out of it earlier."

"Yeah, I'm fine."

A Window to Young Minds

In his room, Allan breathed out slowly. He was lost in his memories.

Visions of his grandfather and him echoed in his memories.

Allan was determined to make this count. The gods had given him a second chance. He was going to win that competition. He was going to make sure his grandpa was in the hospital in time. He was going to fix his life.

The first time, Allan's grandfather had died when he was away at the chess match. Allan was convinced that if he hadn't gone, his grandfather would have survived. Allan could have gotten him to the hospital in time. Now that he had a chance to redo it all, he wasn't sure if he wanted to miss the competition. If he won, he could get into his first-choice college. Allan didn't want to give up that opportunity.

Allan spent the rest of the day practicing, visualizing, and watching chess games. He already knew how his opponents were going to play; he just had to find a way to oppose their strategies. Each time he moved a piece, his grandfather's voice echoed in his head, "Win."

Allan fell asleep that night with the king nestled into his hand.

The next morning Allan woke up early enough to watch the sunrise. He forced himself to stare the sun in the eyes as if he were trying to intimidate it into falling back down into the horizon. It didn't work. The sun rose; the day began.

"Good morning!" Today Allan looked his grandfather straight in the eye. "I'm going to win today."

With that, he gobbled up his omelet and sped out the door. But not before planting the seeds for his second goal of the day.

"Make sure you visit the hospital around three o'clock!"

Allan told his grandfather.

"OK?"

With that, Allan left the house.

Allan fought through every battle at the chess tournament. He used his knight and pawns, and bishops, to tear down defenses. He built his own up with his queen and his rooks. He reached the quarterfinals. The semifinals. The finals. In the end, he held his trophy above his head with pride. He had settled for second place the first time. But this time he had promised to win.

Allan returned home happily. He was so focused on what he had done that he forgot the biggest reason he had fought these many battles.

When he reached home, the house was quiet. "Grandpa?"

No reply. "He's probably in the hospital," Allan remembered. "Oh, well, I'll head over there in a bit."

Allan raced up to his room to put his trophy where it belonged, glittering with the rest if his prizes. But when he flung his door open, the thought barely registered when his saw what was there.

The trophy slipped out of his hands and clattered to the floor.

A Window to Young Minds

The Rendering

Cate Pitterle

(Age: Fifteen)

Life doesn't always happen the way you want it to. For me, it started at the Rendering.

The sky was brilliant red that morning, and the sun's rays pooled on the carriage floor like blood. I shivered in anticipation. Today, finally, was the day where I would redeem my family. *Blood paid in blood*, like the king would say. It was a good statement, and I clung to it.

The carriage was silent, the air static. I looked out through the open window, beholding the metal high-rises that cut into the sky as if winged. We would live here one day, my family and I. We'd rise from the dark alleyways of Probrum Sector, the cramped buildings and smoke-hazed sky, the shame of never fighting for our country. I would change that.

I imagined myself in an ashen battlefield, my sword raised over my head. *I am Sophy of Probrum, hero of Augusta. I am victorious!*

Suddenly the wheels of the carriage screeched to a stop. I jolted from my daydream, turned to the proctor sitting on the seat across from me, and asked, "Why are we stopping?"

The corner of his mouth twitched—to smile or to frown, I didn't know. Probably frown, knowing the high-and-mighty proctors.

"We're at the arena, girl," he said. "For your Rendering?"

He phrased it as a question, and I bit back a sharp retort. *I'm not as dumb as you think I am. And I am certainly stronger.*

Instead I flashed him a wry smile. "I had a feeling, yes. How lovely." The words rolled off my lips, and I giggled falsely. The proctor rolled his eyes and sat back. No doubt he got the same act from the many rich girls who rolled through every year.

The carriage door next to me opened, and the proctor ushered me outside. I leaped down with catlike grace, and the proctor followed, using the handle to step lightly to the ground. It took all my self-control not to sneer.

All around me, carriages stopped to reveal all manner of teenagers. Ahead a girl in a jewel-encrusted jumpsuit flounced to the ground. *It might be hard to move in that*, I thought as I peered at my own plain black one. It was stretchy and cool against my skin. My parents had paid a fortune to get it for me.

We formed up quickly, clustering together in perfect squares. We'd been taught the motion since grade school, and I set my feet in the familiar marching rhythm. *Imagine you're off to fight the Hatiums*, I thought and then smiled. If I succeeded today, I almost certainly would be.

I knew instinctively what weapon I would possess. *A sword.* It'd been my favorite weapon since I could walk; it moved more like an extra arm than a blade.

And when I got my sword, I'd be in possession of a Greater Weapon. I would get a commission from the army, and I would send the paychecks to my family. It would be enough to get them out of poverty. My baby sister would grow up wealthy, in the world of bright red skies, soaring towers, and fresh, clean air. The world of Statum, our capital.

I would win it for her. All it took was a sword.

A Window to Young Minds

***

"The following ceremony is in honor of our dear ruler, His Majesty King August II!" the orator shouted. I stiffened, as did the other teenagers listening.

"Long live the king!" we roared, voices ringing across the stadium.

"Good welcome!" the orator cried again. "Today, young citizens of Augusta, heralds of your sectors, you will prove your worth to our country. You will stand here in the circle and take the weapon that calls out to you and then walk back to your seat. Understand?"

At the ensuing silence, he continued, "If you are worthy to fight in the army—that is, if you are chosen by a Greater Weapon—then you will find out today, in this arena. You will receive the honor of defending our beloved country from the savages of Hatium."

He paused, and I leaned forward in my seat. "Blood paid in blood, young warriors. Good luck."

He took out a list from a pocket and unfolded it on the podium, smoothing the edges against its gold-plated surface.

"When I call your name, you may come and enter the circle. Santos Corbian, Statum Sector!"

I recognized the name. *A good family. Warriors.*

Santos walked down the steps slowly, his steps deliberate. Gold crusted his suit, and it glinted in the red sunlight. He nodded to the orator as he stepped into the circle, and immediately a beam of blinding light hit him. He stood still for a second, his arms outstretched. Then he walked forward as if pulled by some invisible force, toward a dark-wood bow resting on its podium. *A Greater Weapon*. He took it to cheers from his friends in the crowd and then spun around as the light disappeared. He grinned, his teeth flashing, and strutted back to his seat.

"Titus Nordyke, Laeta Sector," was called next. His routine was largely the same as Santos's, as was the routine of "Ara Phalen, Parvus Sector."

The names continued, "Catalina Hisel, Verus"; "Olen Serdo, Magna"; "Rodina"; "Boldery"; and "Alcer." Around the circle, weapons disappeared one by one. A javelin, another bow, a scythe. One unfortunate warrior took a dagger. But not the sword. *Not yet.* "Dena Estel," came next and then, "Galen Holdis, Probrum." The boy next to me rose, his legs shaking. Fear hit me full-on then, clouding my senses.

I'm next. My heart beat a harried rhythm, and I shook my head. *Snap out of it.*

"Sophy Thiara, Probrum."

My breath hitched, and I slowly rose to my feet. I walked to the marching rhythm, and it calmed me. Slowly my confidence returned, and my heart swelled with anticipation. I reached the last step, and my feet hit hard-packed sand, crunching beneath my shoes. I smiled at the orator as I stepped into the circle.

The hum of weapons hit me immediately, soft voices weaving through my ears like patchwork. For a moment, nothing happened.

Then I felt a pull, and I broke into a wide grin. *My sword!* Closing my eyes, I walked toward the pull. Each step felt like I was walking on air. I reached out and wrapped my hand against the soft leather hilt—

My eyes flew open. The hilt wasn't there.

A Window to Young Minds

Grasped in my hand was a tiny device, tipped with a stain of something black. My heart stopped. I didn't recognize it. I didn't know what it was.

The orator turned to me, his mouth open to announce my choice. Instead it clamped shut, and something ugly flashed in his eyes.

Was that fear?

"You...you got the..." he said, voice wavering. He shook his head and turned to face the audience. Petrified, I stared up at the waves of people.

The orator coughed into his megaphone. "Presenting Sophy of Probrum, wielder of the pen!"

***

The next hours flashed by, marked only by rolling carriage wheels and the tang of smoke. My mind was everywhere at once. *I failed.* The thought pounded in my head like the hoofbeats of our carriage's horses. *I failed.* My family would never live in Statum. We were destined only for shame.

A man spoke beside me. "Miss Thiara, we're here."

I snapped out of my daze, and the world came into focus. The man beside me was the proctor from before, and he smiled coldly at me. The carriage stuttered to a stop, and the proctor clamped a hand on my shoulder. I gritted my teeth as pain raced down my arm.

The door swung open, and I gasped. Before me was Statum Castle.

The proctor pulled me to the ground. He landed lightly, and I stumbled as I followed. The castle towered above me, and I stared with wide eyes. Fear shot through me then, sharp

Short Stories by Young Writers

and biting.

Slowly the drawbridge lowered. It was metal, just like the city. Like the castle. Like a sword blade I would never possess and the armor of a military I would never join.

The drawbridge hit the ground, and the sight filled me with dread. I forced back a whimper as the proctor shoved me toward it. *What is happening?* I rested my hands in the crook of my spine, feeling as though a coarse rope had looped its way around them, keeping me prisoner. *But I am still free. Aren't I?*

The orator had told me I was the first pen wielder in a hundred years. I tried to think back that far, but I couldn't. All my history books started fifty years ago, when the war with the Hatium Empire started.

The castle gates swept open with a sigh, and we strode through them. My heart pounded like a war drum. *I am Sophy of Probrum Sector, and I have risen from a girl of a poor family to the hero of Augusta,* I thought. But the words were useless. I was no hero and never would be without a blade at my side. *I am useless.*

Suddenly the proctor leaned down and whispered in my ear, "It seems you're a very special girl, Sophy of Probrum."

I froze, forgetting my feet. The proctor released his grip on my shoulder and circled to face me, a cool smile plastered on his face.

"His Majesty has requested an audience with you. Do not mess it up, *warrior.*"

Terror bled through me, and I whipped my head to him, shocked. "You mean the king—His Majesty—wants to meet with...with me?"

Anger tugged at the proctor's frozen smile and fought to

stay hidden. But his eyes betrayed him. They swam with red-hot fury, and I saw a flash of something else there, too. *Envy?* I smirked at the sight. A proctor of Statum was jealous of me, a poor girl who wielded only a pen.

"Well, it seems I must not be late," I said, giddy sarcasm lacing my voice. "Isn't that right?"

He scoffed and turned away, marching through the arched doorways of the castle. I followed close behind, feeling the magnitude of the moment at last. I settled on my shoulders like armor, heavy and cold, and I straightened under the invisible weight.

Golden cloth hung on every castle wall, with jewel-encrusted metal everywhere the eye could see. I started at the splendor, and shock bled through me like ice. I knew Augusta's rich flaunted their wealth, but I had always imagined the king to be a simple man, too engrossed in his work to care about jewels or gold.

I was wrong. But then again I'd been wrong about a lot lately.

The throne room branched to the right of the foyer, two closed metal doors gleaming at the entrance. A guard stood at either side, and when they saw us, they pulled open the doors, moving with practiced swiftness. The sneering proctor gestured for me to enter. Training took over, and I stepped through the doors with grace, my head down. I longed to look up to where I knew the king sat on his steel throne, but I wasn't so bold. Instead I dropped to my knees, and they hit the floor with a soft thump.

A gentle voice rang out above me.

"Rise, Sophy of Probrum," the king said, and I stood, daring to meet his eyes for the first time. I was expecting an intense gaze, the gaze of a soldier, but his eyes melted into mine like chocolate.

"Sophy Thiara, pen wielder, I need your help."

My breath caught in my throat. "Your Majesty?"

He smiled. "I need you to draft a peace treaty."

***

The trumpets were not of war today. They rang out over the castle grounds, light and uplifting, high notes ringing in my ears. Exhausted of its power, my pen rested in my hand. I stared out at the courtyard, at the thousands of people seated and waiting. The castle walls rose around us, draped with alternating banners: the deep red of Augusta and Hatium's midnight blue.

I stood behind the king as he lifted his own quill above a sheet of beautifully styled print. *My handwriting.* Every word had flowed out of me like water until I'd had a treaty before me.

A burly man sat on the chair to the king's left: the Hatium emperor. He was perched on the edge of the chair, as if he were about to flee, but his hand was firm as he took his quill.

Slowly King August began to sign.

A hush went through the courtyard, even among the journalists who waited with paper and ink in the front row.

The king set his quill down, and the Hatium emperor signed with a few scratches on the paper. He and his entourage were not as savage as I'd been taught to believe, and I smiled. Both our countries were tired of war, so we brought peace instead.

The trumpets blared again, a solemn tune. Both rulers rose, and the crowd erupted into cheers. My gaze drifted to

A Window to Young Minds

my family, all beaming in the front row with my sister in my mother's arms. My heart swelled with warmth at the sight.

As I started to clap, I whispered a familiar mantra under my breath, "I am Sophy of Probrum, and I have risen. I am victorious."

The Day I Lost My Memory

Soumya Shenoy

(Age: Ten)

I am Sarah. I am eighteen years old and love horseback riding. Every weekend my best friend, Lizzy, and I get dressed and take a ride in the countryside. My dad is always telling me to ride with a helmet. But I am so good that the chances of me falling off are one in a million (according to my calculations).

Dingdong. That's Lizzy. Time to ride.

We get to the trail, and Lizzy asks, "Hey, do you want to try jumping over that huge rotting log?"

"Piece of cake," I answer confidently.

Soon after about fifteen minutes of trotting, we see the log. I go first. We have the perfect takeoff and landing, but as we hit the ground, a huge snake slithers past. My horse freaks out and bucks. I fly out of the saddle and bang my head on a log. The last thing I remember is Lizzy screaming to me to keep my eyes open. Then everything goes black.

I wake up with a bunch of strangers looking at me. They keep saying that they are relieved to know I am OK, but I don't understand why. My head is swimming with questions. I black out again.

I wake to find that an older man is hugging me and saying, "Sarah."

When I finally have enough power to speak, I whisper,

"Who is Sarah?"

The man hugging me gasps. The lady in the white coat stops smiling. The other man with a weird metal thing hanging around his neck says something about me losing my memory.

What memory? How did I lose it? What is going on? My head swarms with questions.

There is a knock on the door, and a teenage girl comes in. She has tears running down her cheeks. The doctor whispers something to her, and her eyes fill with sympathy. I feel like I am supposed to remember her, but I just don't. I feel like I am an alien from outer space. Everyone leaves the room, leaving just her and me. She sits down on the bed and says that she is my best friend, Lizzy. She tries to remind me of all the things we supposedly did together. She talks about horseback riding and sleepovers. None of these things seems familiar.

I start talking to her. She was my best friend, so I must have some trust in her.

"What is going on?" I whisper. "Who was that man who was hugging me and saying, 'Sarah'? Who is Sarah?"

"That man is your father, and you are Sarah. You are eighteen years old. You love horseback riding. You live on a ranch, and you have your own horse you named Marshmallow."

"Oh, OK," I say slowly. "But if I have a father, where is my mother?"

Lizzy is silent, and then she whispers, "Your mother died two years ago, of cancer."

Waves of grief wash over me, I can't even remember my own mother's death. How sad is that? When the pain subsides, Lizzy says that I should rest; it has been a long day. I snuggle into the bed and close my eyes. I can hear Lizzy closing the door as she walks out. I smile. I can see why Lizzy was my best friend.

The next morning, I wake up, and I see my father standing at the bed stand. I stretch my arms up and yawn.

"Hi, Daddy," I say in a sleepy tone.

"Morning, sunshine. Are you ready to go home?" he says cheerfully.

I freeze.

"What home?" I manage to stutter.

"Oh, Lizzy didn't tell you," he responds with a nervous smile.

My voice is shaky. "I just got used to the hospital, and now my world is going to get even bigger and more confusing."

I start crying like a six-year-old, and then I remember I don't even know what I was like as a six-year-old. That just makes me cry even harder.

Soon the tears stop flowing, and I start packing my belongings. We are in the car, and after a five-minute drive, we pull into the driveway of the house.

I step inside. It is a huge house. The wood is polished, and there are pictures hanging everywhere. The stable has five horses. I guess Marshmallow is the white mare. She seems to remember me, but I have no connection to her. I know I should be happy to be home, the place where I spent my childhood, but it all seems so strange. I would feel the same just walking into any old house.

Every day Lizzy comes by and helps me remember something about my childhood. I spend the day looking at

A Window to Young Minds

family albums, trying to remember. I keep a box of tissues handy just in case.

It is Friday night, and I am ready for bed, pajamas on and teeth brushed. I pray every night in the hope of getting my memory back, but tonight is different. I take a picture of my mother and hang it in my room. Then I climb into bed.

Tonight I don't pray. I dream. I dream of getting my memory back. I dream of having sleepovers with Lizzy when I was six. I dream of being thrown off my horse and banging my head on a log. I dream of all the memories I had lost. They are coming back to me flooding my brain. I dream of my memories all through the night.

I wake up and get dressed. It's the weekend, time to go riding with Lizzy. When I get down the stairs, I see Lizzy and my dad. They are staring at me with my riding boots and gloves on.

"What? I say. "It's the weekend. I'm supposed to go riding with Lizzy."

Slowly my dad asks, "Sarah, when is your birthday?"

"June sixteenth," I say, rolling my eyes. I start walking toward the door to get Marshmallow. I freeze and slowly turn around.

"Dad!" I say excitedly.

"Yes, Sarah," he says, grinning.

Lizzy is smiling from ear to ear.

We all hop into the car and rush to the doctor. After a few long tests, it is confirmed; I have my memory back. Lizzy and I squeal and hug each other.

This is no doubt the happiest day of my life.

Promise

Huda Haque

(Age: Thirteen)

I roll over in my sleep, blinking away the hazy feeling from my eyes. The room is still dark, and my house-pod window displays *Night* in neon-green lettering. I don't need to be awake now, but the feeling of thirst tugs at my throat. So I get up and walk toward the water station in my house pod.

All of a sudden, a soft rustling catches my keen ears, and I jerk up from my glass of water. A scream is seconds away from escaping me when the tall intruder in front of me flings his gloved hands around my mouth. I can barely make out his face in the darkness.

"Please," he begs, "don't say anything! I'll be gone before you know it. I haven't taken anything."

Frozen with shock, I slowly and stupidly nod. The robber doesn't look armed, and besides I don't have access to any weapon to hurt him quickly. His voice isn't that of a crazed murderer, either. For these reasons, I let the robber silently slide out of the house pod, and I go back to bed.

As I drift back into my sleep, I comfort myself by thinking, *That was probably a dream.*

The next day, my window screeches, "Alarm!" at the top of its robotic voice. I always set it to this voice so that I know I'll get up, no matter what. After getting dressed, I head downstairs, still replaying my encounter with the robber last night. Where could he be now? Did he lie about not taking

A Window to Young Minds

anything?

The thoughts circling my mind are cut off abruptly when my father and mother greet me.

"Did you sleep well?" they ask in a monotone, like they always do.

I say yes, because what else can I possibly tell them? They surely wouldn't believe me if I say, "Oh, sort of. A masked person begged me to not say anything about his break-in, but I am anyway letting you know!"

They smile that normal, adult smile that doesn't quite reach the eyes and leave for work.

My parents take the Router, the transportation system that every person in our town must take. If not, rumor has it that the government will isolate the person from his or her family members.

I tell myself not to ponder the idea too much. We've all been taught not to question; the adults at the government know what's best for all. And so I go to school, like on all normal days.

The time is 3:10 p.m., and after getting off of the Router, eager to get inside, I hastily thrust my hand toward the house-pod scanner.

"House pod DBT. Member number three. Accepted," the monotonous voice says, like always.

At school we get a lot of work, and I want to finish it soon so that I can play with Maribel, our neighbor. She's nine, but she's like a little sister.

After I am done at school, I'm transported inside my house pod and fumble with my books, almost dropping them, at the sight in front of me. My mother and father are here, which isn't the alarming part, but there is a third person next to them. A tall man, with jet-black hair and very green

Short Stories by Young Writers

eyes. It's the robber from last night! I'm sure of it!

My father is the first to speak. "Thea, the young man here is Alexander. He's a good friend from work."

My father smiles and turns to Alexander.

"Hello," Alexander says, and now I am more positive than ever that it's the same person. The voice sounds exactly the same. I look at Alexander, and his eyes convey desperation and a pleading look. I can tell my parents that he broke into our house pod, I really can. But should I? Somehow I don't feel like Alexander is a bad person.

"Hello," I say back, smiling as if I've never seen him before.

I follow my parents and Alexander to the sitting room. The table conjures up food, and my father motions for Alexander to take some.

"No, thank you, I already had food," he says in a polite voice that has a hidden edge to it.

My parents raise their eyebrows.

"Are you sure?" my mother asks.

"Yes, it's written in my food log. Shall I show it to you?" he replies firmly.

I instinctively reach for my food log in my pocket. It must be kept with all citizens at all times. At school we learned that the reason is because the government wants to make sure all of us eat the given food and stay healthy.

"There's no need for that." My father chuckles. It sounds odd, because neither of my parents laugh often.

"Now, Thea, why don't you finish your schoolwork? We have to talk about work business."

I take that as my obvious cue to leave and go upstairs. The thought of wanting to play with Maribel escapes me, and I think about Alexander. If he's friends with my parents, could

A Window to Young Minds

he really be a robber? But why would he want to rob his friends' house in the first place?

I'm interrupted by a knock at my door. I open it slowly, and standing there is Alexander. He looks very nervous.

"I have to tell you something," he says hurriedly. "I don't have much time; your parents will be wondering what's taking me so long.

"I know you saw me last night, and I know you must be thinking that I'm some crazy robber. But I promise you I am not. I am one of the few people who are unaffected by the government's brainwashing poison. They put the poison in everything, from the Router to the food. It gets rid of people's free thinking.

"I found out, and I started avoiding the Router, thinking it would help free me. I discovered that I was immune to it anyway, but before that, they took my siblings and my parents. I only came to your house pod to get something, anything, that could bribe them to let my family go. And to tell you, Thea, that you are one of the Immunes, too."

My mother calls up from downstairs, "Alexander?"

He quickly closes my door and heads downstairs, and then he continues chatting with my parents nonchalantly, like he hadn't just dumped life-changing information on the thirteen-year-old girl upstairs.

I slide down to the floor and silently look at myself in the mirror for a couple of minutes. We've been brainwashed? What else is poisoned around me? The carpet? The air? Is this why all the other people smile so robotically and speak in the same, monotone voice? And why am I special?

My eyes bore into the reflection of the mirror as I softly ask myself the question that I know will define me for the years to come.

Is being one of the Immunes going to give me a purpose in this world?

I go through the rest of my day normally, trying my best not to let on what I have learned. My parents are brainwashed, but that sure doesn't mean I want to get isolated from them.

When I go to school the next day, I carefully listen to everything that our teacher says and try to listen for holes in the story. And I do hear some. Everything that is required for the citizens has the same exact reason. To make you strong and healthy. No other further explanation, no further details. I hear those two words so many times over the course of the school day, and each time they form even a bigger blatant lie staring me in the face.

I look around the classroom pod, trying to spot any facial expression on any of my classmates' faces, trying to find out if any of them may belong to the Immunes. Now that I've realized that I am one of the Immunes, anyone I talk to seems so blank, so empty. There have to be other Immunes out there.

I come home from school, and Alexander is here again, much to my surprise.

"Alexander and I have more work to do," my father says.

I nod slowly and head up to my room again.

After about an hour, Alexander knocks on my door.

"You're in luck. The Immunes' monthly meeting is taking place at midnight. Try your best to make it," he whispers urgently.

"Wait!" I say, after realizing something. "But where is it?"

"You'll find it. Just remember, look for the blue in an unexpected place," he says mysteriously and goes back downstairs.

I rack my brain in confusion, trying to think of what he

A Window to Young Minds

may have possibly meant. Blue? All I know about blue is that it is the opposite of orange. The orange is the color of the government symbol. Thus the orange is also the color of the entire Router station. My best bet is to go there and look for the blue.

I quickly set a soft alarm to 11:50 p.m., hoping it will not wake up my parents in the night. A strange feeling of anticipation and excitement fills me. I will hopefully get to meet more Immunes!

A whisper fills my room, and I hear, "Alarm," being said.

I quickly jump out of bed, having been sleeping secretly in regular clothes. I swiftly go downstairs and set the house-pod system to mute so that no one will hear my exit. After getting out of there, I run to my Router station, which is at the end of my neighborhood. The whole place is covered with streaks of orange, and I desperately look for something blue.

Just as I'm about to give up and go home, I spot a blue crystal near the back of the station and sprint toward it. There are no directions, so I quickly jab at it, as it's already 11:58 p.m. My feet drop, and my hands flail as I go down into an opening underneath me, almost floating, with only about one-fifth of the gravity in effect. I close my eyes and pray that I don't die in this underground place.

After a short time, I feel the comfort of land beneath my feet and dare to open my eyes. I now see thirty to forty people, some older than others, some wearing armor. My eyes skitter over them, trying to find someone I know, and Alexander comes up to me.

"You made it!" he says, smiling.

"Yes, I did, but what is this place?" I ask, out of breath.

Out of the corner of my eye, I see, of all people, Maribel. Glad to see more than one person I know, I eagerly wave at her.

"There'll be time for socializing later," Alexander tells me. "We have to get through our meeting quickly. There's a reason why we can only have these once a month and not every week."

Through the meeting, my eyes widen at all the knowledge that I discover. There's a memorial for all of the Immunes who have been killed, and just looking at it gives me chills. But all of this fills me with an inner drive, too. I want to help those who have been wronged and help give back the citizens their free thinking.

So I make a promise to myself. I won't let my gift of being an Immune just pass me by. I have to make this world better with it.

Ninety Years Later

I lie down on my bed, my breath coming in short rasps. Maribel and my other longtime friends stand next to me, along with my husband, children, and grandchildren.

"You'll be fine, Thea. You just need some rest. You're a hundred and three years old. You've been fine for this long; don't worry!" Maribel says, smiling.

But I can see there's a lot of hesitation and anxiety behind those words. My family, my blood relatives, and the others, they all smile worriedly.

"Don't tell me not to worry. I've known this was coming for me for a long time. I want you all not to worry. I love you all so very much," I say, my voice still somewhat strong even after all these years.

Speaking of *all these years*, I've had a wonderful life. Under my eventual leadership, the Immunes were able to get rid of the poison and get back all those who were isolated from their families. No one was brainwashed any longer, including my parents.

At this point I have nothing left to prove, nothing left to do. The last thing I see are the faces of people I've grown so close to over the years fade into that familiar Immune blue.

I think to myself, *I've fulfilled my promise.*

The Black Umbrella

Sonia Birla

(Age: Thirteen)

Dark-gray smudges of wool filled the sky. A startlingly low rumble rang loud in the cool spring air, and the sky roared with satisfaction. The rainfall sounded like a mob of angry bees. Drizzles turned into cannon fires, barraging everything in their way.

That was the Monday morning Samantha faced. She managed to fix her makeup, juggle her bags, grab her black umbrella, and slam the door shut with no time to spare.

Samantha worked at a small diner in the middle of the city. The diner got a fair amount of business, but her boss was strict about punctuality. A few minutes late, and she would have to work overtime. Today she had to leave extra early. Her car was in the repair shop, so she had to walk—or run—to get to the diner on time.

The dissatisfaction showed on her face. *Almost there*, she told herself, clutching her umbrella a centimeter above her head.

Samantha rushed by a small grocery store, where a woman stood in the entrance, one hand on a stroller and the other holding three bags of groceries. No umbrella. She looked up at the sky and put her hand out to catch the icy drops. *I'll just wait it out*, she decided, leaning back against the rough brick wall.

A Window to Young Minds

Nicole usually liked rain, but today it was exhausting to keep her three-month-old baby snuggled tightly in his blue blanket while trying to buy groceries at the same time. Despite the difficulties, it would take more than some lousy weather to phase her.

Samantha almost walked away from Nicole and her baby, and normally she wouldn't have given her a second thought; she was going to be late for work, but she was feeling different this morning. Samantha turned around and approached Nicole. Without words, Samantha grabbed Nicole's bags and replaced them with her umbrella. Then she pulled off her belt and used it to tie the plastic bags to the stroller. Samantha gave a tug to make sure it was secure and nodded at her handiwork. Then less than thirty seconds later, she ran down the pavement, using her purse to cover her head.

Samantha didn't know who this lady was, but she felt like helping. The hero in her came out. She was a bit worried about the woman; it was supposed to rain all day. How long was she going to stand there? Samantha's split-second decision didn't leave room for introductions.

Nicole was surprised. She looked down at the purple belt, looked up at the umbrella, and watched Samantha run down the street, her clacking heels louder than the rain. *Thank you*, she thought. Smiling at her sleeping baby in the stroller, she turned to walk down the other way.

Nicole had to take the bus to get home, a ten-minute ride. At the bus stop, she stood beside a man in jeans and a baggy plaid shirt. He had a faint stubble resting on his chin, which he rubbed every few minutes.

"Noah," he said, introducing himself when he noticed her looking at him.

Short Stories by Young Writers

"Nicole," came the reply, "and this is Julia." She gestured to her baby, who was sound asleep in her stroller.

"Nice to meet you." He smiled at Julia as if she were the best thing on the planet.

Noah didn't have an umbrella, but he didn't seem to mind the rain dripping down his face. It did nothing to wash off his sunny smile. He looked like he had just won the lottery. Noah's eyes anxiously flitted to his watch every few seconds, but his smile was unwavering.

"Where are you going?" Nicole asked in an effort to make small talk.

"The hospital."

"Hospital?" Nicole's voice squeaked toward the end.

"My wife is having a baby!" His voice was laced with excitement, and he looked like he was forcing himself to stand still.

"Congratulations!" Nicole replied, smiling at his euphoria.

Soon enough, a bus pulled up to the stop.

"Bus four, that's me!" Nicole said. She thought for a moment before handing the man the umbrella. "You can't catch a cold before the baby arrives!"

She smiled before picking up her baby and folding the stroller. Nicole was on the bus and out of the rain a moment later.

Noah watched the bus roll away with puffs of black exhaust. The handle of the black umbrella Nicole had pushed into his hands was still warm from her tight grasp. Noah's smile grew a little brighter as he watched his own bus rumble down the street.

"Bus eight!" Noah cheered to himself.

The bus doors opened, letting out warm air from inside.

Noah waited for the passengers to get off before boarding himself. Four passengers got off, three of whom had umbrellas. They quickly opened them and scurried away. The fourth person to get off the bus held nothing but a small briefcase. He looked uncertainly at the sky and slowly got off the bus as he tried to cover his head with his bag.

Noah didn't have to think twice. He handed the man his black umbrella and boarded the bus. Noah settled into his seat and smiled as he watched the man walk away with the umbrella.

Quin had to get to work. He was almost late; the first shift would be ending soon, and he would have to take over at noon. He checked his watch, 11:54 a.m. He began running, because his boss was prickly about being late. Quin was unsure what had compelled the man to give the umbrella to him, but nonetheless he was grateful. Now his boss couldn't get fussy about him leaving watery footprints all over the floor.

He passed Greg's Groceries. *Almost there*. 11:59 a.m. Quin reached his work, the Downtown Diner. He had no time to lose. He closed his umbrella and entered the diner, breathless and dry.

"Hey, Sam," he said, nodding to his coworker.

"Hi, Quin."

Samantha was sitting at one of the tables near the front of the diner and looking out through the glass door blankly.

"Something wrong?" Quin asked.

"I don't have an umbrella." She sighed.

Samantha had forgotten that she would need her umbrella on the way home. She resisted the urge to stomp her feet in frustration. Her usual lack of forethought made her want to

Short Stories by Young Writers

scream.

"Here, take mine." Quin handed her the umbrella. "It's not really mine; some dude on the street gave it to me."

"Some dude on the street?" She accepted the umbrella and held it tightly in her fingers.

"This is my umbrella!" She looked up in disbelief, ready to ask Quin fifteen different questions at once. But Quin was already gone.

Samantha stood in disbelief. She was holding the same umbrella she had given to a woman and her child hours earlier. She opened her umbrella and exited the diner with a smile.

The rain finally became a light drizzle on Samantha's way home. She closed her umbrella and looked up at the brightening sky. Umbrellas closed. Windows and doors opened, and suddenly people were outside, enjoying the sunshine. Through the mist, Samantha saw an arc of color. A rainbow decorated the sky.

Escaping the Rising Storm

Logan M. Egle

(Age: Fourteen)

*T*he lush island of Lothbrok used to be a place of freedom and happiness. This all changed when the demons from the north sailed to the island, bearing black sails and beast heads carved from wood hung upon the bows of their long ships. They beached their war boats on the shores of black sand and ravaged Lothbrok. They burned and pillaged their way through the island, taking whatever would fill their pockets and bags most lucratively. By the end of the third day, there was all but naught left of the once-beautiful island. All except a farmer's son, a fisherman's son, a cobbler's daughter, and their faithful mutt.

"Push!" Osbert, the fisherman's son, yelled over the rain.

With that final attempt, the three teenagers managed to get the rowboat into the water. They all jumped in, grabbed oars, and began to row with all their might. Panther, the dog, whined.

"Hey, hey, it'll be all right," Osbert said, rubbing the dog's head.

"God have mercy," said Mikael, the farmer's son, looking back to their small town. Even through the darkness and rain, he could see smoke and fire dancing in the black sky above their home. AEthelflaed, the cobbler's daughter, began to cry.

"Come on, AEthel," Osbert said, "we must keep rowing, or they'll catch us."

"How could they have done this? The north continent has never posed any threat," she replied.

"All I know is that we must keep moving," Mikael said helplessly. "We have to get to the south continent. There we can start anew and carry on our families' names."

Hearing this, she stopped crying and started rowing again.

They then rowed for what seemed an eternity and decided that they were safe. They slept.

Mikael was the first to awake. The sea beneath and the sky above were calm and quiet, like two big blue walls covering the world in between. He looked up at the cloud-dotted sky and was thankful that the storm had passed without causing them or the boat any harm. He bent over and looked inside the wet sack that held the few belongings they had brought with them. The bread was soaked, so he set it on one of the seats as an attempt to dry it.

His commotion woke up the others as well.

"Did we bring any food?" Osbert asked.

"A little. We're going to have to share," responded Mikael.

He poured the sack's contents onto the floor of the boat. They counted one wheel of hard cheese, two full water skins, a few coins, a pile of wet clothes, and the bread that was still sun drying.

"This isn't going to last very long," Æthelflaed said.

They then broke a piece of the cheese off and divided it into thirds and ate.

"What about Panther?" she asked.

"I don't know," Mikael said thoughtfully. "This is a sea, so there's gotta be fish somewhere."

He saw a fishing net at one end of the boat. Trying not to fall overboard, he got up and walked the length of the small boat and grabbed the net.

"This should do," he said.

"I know how to use it. My pa taught me," Osbert said.

Mikael handed over the net, and Osbert explained how to get it ready and demonstrated how to throw it into the water.

"So after the net is in the water, we wait," Osbert said. "Watch for the rope to tug, and then we'll know if we got anything."

They waited for half an hour before AEthelflaed noticed the rope pull back a little and then more, and then the rope pulled until it almost fell out of the boat. Osbert quickly grabbed it and called for help to drag the net on board.

"We might have just gotten a school full of 'em," Osbert said in through his teeth.

The three of them pulled first half of the net, and then Panther barked at the thing that was inside. With another heave, the net slid onto the floor, spilling numerous little gray fish.

"Gray fins," said Osbert. He caught his breath. "My pa and his friends used to bring barrels of these over the mountain and sell them in Efluv."

Efluv was the largest city on Lothbrok, located right in the center.

"How do they taste?" Mikael asked.

"When you roast 'em over a fire and peel the skin off, it's like Valhalla in the flesh of a fish."

"We don't have a fire," AEthelflaed said.

"That doesn't mean we can't eat 'em." Osbert responded.

"I'm not going to eat a raw fish," AEthel said as Osbert put a few in her hand. "They're still alive!" she squealed.

"Don't worry. The bones are small. and the meat tastes just like chicken," Osbert teased, ignoring the fact that the fishes were still alive. He then took a fish in his hand, twisted off its head, and ate it as whole. A look a pure delight spread across his face.

Mikael shrugged and did the same. Panther had already eaten no fewer than ten by now.

AEthelflaed took a fish in her hand, closed her eyes, plugged her nose, and took a small bite. She spat it all out the next moment, gagging. Mikael and Osbert laughed.

After finishing their meal, they began to row again.

Three days had passed since they fled. Their water skins had run dry, and the fish had become scarce. It was around noon when AEthelflaed stood up and scanned the horizon.

"Hey, guys, look at this," she said, pointing in a direction. They all wearily got up and looked. They saw black flags in the distance.

"Northmen," Mikael said to no one.

"Come on. We have to get rowing," Osbert frantically said.

Panther sat up, not knowing what was going on. They began to row. Mikael prayed.

"How did they know we left the island?" AEthel asked.

"Ours is the only boat left other than theirs—so they might have realized that a few of us had gotten away."

After an hour of rowing, they stopped because they simply couldn't continue. They were hungry, thirsty, and exhausted. The ship was closer now. The group knew that they were doomed to the will of the Northmen. Mikael still prayed.

"Mikael, stop praying. It's useless," Osbert said, gazing into the darkening sky. The farmer's son refused to listen.

"What now?" asked AEthelflaed.

"I think our best bet is to wait for the ship to come and then put up as best fight we can," Osbert proposed.

"So just give up? After all we've done to survive, you just

want to give up?" AEthelflaed said with slight irritation.

"No, I said we make one final stand. We might die, but so what? At least we'll die knowing that we gave it our best shot," Osbert clarified his stand.

She couldn't believe him. She picked up her oar and started to row again. It did little, but she wasn't going to give in to Osbert's radical beliefs.

The black sails were less than a mile away.

"Give it up already! It's useless," Osbert sulked, back on the seat

"Osbert Gedrinson, I've known you for fifteen years, and you have never given up so easily. So stop being like this and help me!" AEthelflaed screamed.

Osbert decided that he might as well try. He picked up his oar and started to row with her. Just as he did, the sky darkened, and the wind picked up, pushing them south. Behind them, where the Northmen's ship was, a whirlpool began to form and trapped their enemy's ship.

Mikael stopped praying and helped the two row. The sky began to clear up after few minutes. Their enemy's ship was now much farther behind. Therefore the group decided to rest.

It was only a few minutes before Panther looked off the prow and started barking. Osbert got up to see what he was barking at.

He looked back with a look of disbelief on his face. "Come and look at this!" he yelled.

They hadn't realized until now that the shore of the south continent was merely two miles away. AEthelflaed wept passionately—but with the tears of relief and joy. The three came back to reality when Osbert uttered a loud call to row as hard as they could.

As they approached the shore, Osbert could see crowds of men on the shore. Some of them were soldiers in military uniforms with weapons, while the others were peasants.

The three beached their boat and sighed in relief. Before they could put down their oars, the soldiers lifted them out of the boat and escorted them to the city center. The soldiers asked them countless questions. They disregarded the questions.

"Did you see the ship?" croaked Osbert. He looked back, but it was gone.

"Yes, the black flagged one," the soldier said, pushing through the crowds. "I believe a great war is coming to this land, and to tell you the truth, I'm afraid."

Paper Airplanes

Debra Adamolekun

(Age: Sixteen)

*H*e was waiting for the old soul trapped in the dreamer's body. Technically speaking, she was late beyond reason. But that was OK; time couldn't hold her any more than Callum ever could.

His breath hitched with just the thought of her. He knew he would wait in this deserted park till he turned to dust, granted he even had the slightest chance of inhaling the jasmine in her hair. He'd stay put on this swing set till the end of eras if only to stare into those rich cocoa eyes till he turned to stone.

Suddenly it hit him. Literally. A paper airplane gliding on the wind hit Callum smack in the nose, the failed aircraft crash landing into his lap. He had a moment of silence for the imaginary paper people aboard during the accident and unraveled the notebook paper, revealing a rushed yet artful scrawl:

Come over tonight if you dare.
Shay

Callum sprinted out the park gates for his secondhand bike as his heart picked up speed, which had nothing to do with the fact that he was running. He was enthralled by just the thought of seeing her. A smile that even the most cynical of people would call *lovestruck* adorned the teenager's face as he pedaled to the end of the street, where she and her enormous house stood waiting.

"I almost thought you wouldn't show, but then again you are in love with me," she said.

Callum flew off his bike at her bold statement and crashed into the pavement. In an instant, she was at his side, swallowing her surprise to help him back to his feet.

"Wow, Mr. Harris, I wasn't expecting such a reaction. I must be funnier than I give myself credit for."

"Hilarious, really." Callum laughed, despite the ebbing pain starting at his knees.

Shay checked her watch, a frown playing at her lips. "C'mon, there's something I need to tell you."

When she grasped Callum's hand, he was hers.

Shay pulled him through the front door like his first steps into her sanctuary was nothing.

The structure was luxurious but lacking in something Callum couldn't quite put his finger on. They clambered up the stairs and into a room at the end of the hall.

The interior of the room was dark and roomy, made seemingly more so by the strange lack of furniture. The walls were bare, with the exception of lights that imitated the stars. Candles stood gravely on the windowsill, emitting a calming herbal scent, and lying on the white carpet floor was a speaker and her nice winter coat.

"This is your room?" Callum wondered out loud as he inspected the grooves of a candle more closely. Shay closed the door behind them.

"You like it?" she asked.

The room may have been dark, but her smile was clear as day.

A Window to Young Minds

"Sure, but like…where's your bed?"

He ventured to the middle of the bedroom.

"Are you admitting to me that you're secretly Edward Cullen?" Callum asked.

Whenever Shay laughed, her head tilted back. This time it nearly hit the floor.

"Are you admitting to me that you've willingly watched the *Twilight* movies?" Shay asked.

"Read the books, actually," Callum muttered. "But anyway you wanted to tell me something?"

Shay's face fell once again, leaving Callum with an uneasy feeling about the news.

"I do," she said. "But how about a little recap first?"

"A recap?"

"Of every night we've spent at the park, all in about ten minutes. I thought I'd bring the park in here tonight." She couldn't seem to bring herself to look at him.

Even though the lights and herbal scent now made sense, Callum was still lost on the whole *recap* thing. So naturally he asked no questions.

"Ten minutes on the clock."

Her smile in that next moment was enough to make every single doubt he'd ever had vanish. It was a smile that set light to her eyes like a fire kindled out of eternal darkness.

Shay sat on the floor, her pale legs stretched out in comfort. She said, "A typical night at the park. First I'd arrive awfully late."

He tentatively joined her on the floor, careful not to touch her. He said, "And I'd remind you that I was just awfully early."

"I'd complain about my current boyfriend and the latest way he'd hurt me." She placed her hand on the floor, in the small space between them.

"And I'd promise to beat him to the ground if I could." After only mild hesitation, Callum's own hand was covering hers.

Callum continued, "I'd complain about the bullies at school locking me in my own locker."

"And I'd actually beat them to the ground."

They laughed unanimously, not because Shay couldn't beat them to the ground but because of the looks they imagined on everyone's faces when she did.

"In a quiet moment, I'd ask you who invented the stars…" Shay trailed off.

"And I'd answer, 'The people looking at them.'"

On cue, their hands intertwined, they looked to the stars decorating the otherwise plain wall.

That was only until Shay's hand slipped from his grasp, leaving Callum desperately trying not to care.

"I'd ask if you'd found any new music…," Shay said.

Callum's iPod was already out of his pocket. He said, "And I'd pull up the playlist I compiled the night before."

Shay took the iPod and stood up to retrieve one of the objects from the floor. She said, "I'd hook it up to my speakers."

"And my inner thoughts would pour out for us like rain."

Tonight the music selection was chiller than their usual rock, the darkness, candles, and haunting melodies creating the illusion of a dream. In a way, that was just what it was.

"No matter what was playing, I'd ask you to dance," Shay said. Shay offered Callum her hand like a true gentleman.

"And I'd insist that the man is supposed to ask," he replied.

He accepted her hand, curtsying with his invisible skirt.

A Window to Young Minds

Shay suppressed a giggle. "Then under my breath, I'd ask, 'What man?'"

"What?"

"Nothing."

The unlikely pair swayed to the music, so close yet so far away. During the climax of the song, Shay removed her hands from his shoulders to receive her winter coat from the floor and slipped it on. She found her rightful place across from Callum and placed her hands behind his neck.

"By now you would have attempted to dip me," Shay said.

Callum blushed profusely and replied, "Just to get caught on your coat."

Sure enough, that's exactly what happened.

"Your face would turn impressively red." She untangled Callum and slung her now-useless coat to the ground.

"And I'd think of every insecure thought I could muster." He closed his eyes as his own thoughts taunted him. "I'd wonder why I'm such a klutz."

"And I'd wonder why your burning face looks so adorable in the moonlight."

"I'd remember that you're taller than me." He stared at her shoeless feet.

"And I'd think of how beautiful your accent is." She tilted his head up so that he'd have to look at her.

"I'd wonder why the Shay Monique Garner would want anything to do with me."

"And I'd wonder which star I should be thanking for giving me you."

The song ended. The room was completely silent except for the sound of their heavy breath mingling. The pair stood completely still, their reddened faces inches apart, arms still wrapped around each other. Their eyes still trying to decipher each other's heart.

"When will you fall in love with me?" Callum blurted out, no longer sticking to the script.

Shay was taken aback but still answered confidently, "When I'm forty-five years old."

He had expected a lot of things but definitely not this strange, specific answer.

"Why?"

"Because that's the golden age of a midlife crisis."

Callum looked at her so intently that she couldn't hold his gaze.

"You don't believe in love," he remembered, his voice reduced to a whisper.

"And I don't see how on earth you could!" she replied.

Callum pressed his lips against hers, standing on his tippy toes to do so. He felt everything he could ever imagine in the way their mouths connected. And for a moment, she may have even kissed back, but all too soon Shay Monique Garner was pulling away, fresh tears shining in her eyes.

"You need to go," she said.

In the utter desperation induced by the wreckage of his own heart, he asked the sole question he would come to regret many times afterward.

"Are you mad enough to love me now?"

———

Callum faced his bathroom mirror and prepared for bed by painstakingly bringing a brush through his hair. The single paper airplane Shay had managed to hide in his curls littered the sink. The folded notebook paper contained what she had wanted to tell him. The three words that changed his life forever.

I'm moving away.

The Mystery of Mr. Linden's Library

Soumya Shenoy

(Age: Ten)

*J*amie couldn't believe it! She had lived in California all her life, and now she was moving to this small city in Jacksonville, Ohio. She had heard that the population of this place was very small!

It's probably so small because nobody wants to live here, she thought.

In Sunnyvale, California, she had many friends whom she had known for years. Of course it wasn't her choice to leave; it was her mother's. She didn't refuse because she knew that her mom was still upset about her dad. Jamie had asked her mom why they had to move to Ohio about a *million* times! Her mother gave her the same answer every time.

"Jamie, we cannot afford paying this rent anymore after..." Then her mom just stopped.

One day when Jamie came home from exploring the city, she found her mom waiting for her. Her mom told her that she had a surprise. She had found a library that was only five blocks away from their apartment. For the first time in months, a smile crept onto Jamie's face. Her mother knew that books were the one thing that Jamie cherished more than anything.

Immediately Jamie asked, "Can I go there right now?"

A Window to Young Minds

"Sure," her mom replied.

Jamie dashed out the door and ran to the library. She skidded to a stop when she got past the library door. The library was very small, compared to all the ones she had been to in California. There were old-fashioned brick walls, with large brass chandeliers hanging from the ceiling.

The librarian looked up through his thick glasses. He was a tall man with slick black hair.

He calmly welcomed her, "Hello, I am Mr. Linden. Can I help you?"

Suddenly Jamie became shy, "I am Jamie, and I just moved here. I was wondering if there were any books you could recommend."

"I recommend *The Secret Garden*. Have you read it?" replied Mr. Linden.

"Um…no, I haven't. Where is it?" Jamie said softly.

"I'll show you where it is, but before I do, you must promise to obey the only rule in this library. No matter what, you may never take any of the books out of the library."

"What? What kind of library doesn't let you take the books out of it?" Jamie muttered.

The librarian frowned and replied, "Sorry, but that's the rule."

Jamie spent hours trying to finish the book. At last the librarian got up. He tapped her on the shoulder and quietly whispered, "I am sorry to disappoint you, but it is time for the library to close."

Jamie looked up at the clock. She was supposed to be home by now! But she desperately wanted to finish this interesting book! Jamie didn't know if she would get the book the next day, because somebody else might have it. She really

Short Stories by Young Writers

didn't want to break the rules, but how else would she finish the book?

The library had so many books, Mr. Linden probably wouldn't notice the loss of one little book? She slid the book in her backpack, and then without making any eye contact, she said good-bye to Mr. Linden.

After dinner Jamie rushed upstairs to her room and read until she fell asleep with the book still in her arms. She had not realized that she had left the book open. Within few minutes after she was asleep, vines emerged from the book and started growing steadily. The next morning when Jamie woke up, she found that the vines had wrapped around her bed stand. She threw the blanket off and saw that the vines had wrapped around her ankle, too. Jamie ripped the vines off her ankle. She quickly pulled them, and they unraveled off the bed stand. She threw the book into her empty closet and closed the door swiftly. In a hurry, she didn't notice that the book was lying open on the closet floor. Luckily there was nothing in the closet except for the book and her secret stash of candy.

"Jamie, are you OK?" Jamie's mom called.

"Yeah!" Jamie yelled back. Jamie brushed her teeth and then ran downstairs for breakfast.

While Jamie was eating her breakfast, her mom asked, "I have some errands to run. Do you mind spending an hour or two in the library?"

Jamie gobbled up the rest of her pancakes and headed for the library. She walked in and greeted Mr. Linden with a warm smile. Surprisingly he didn't smile back.

Instead he inquired, "A copy of *The Secret Garden* is missing from the library. Do you have any idea where it could be?"

A Window to Young Minds

Jamie shook her head.

"At least we still have another copy of it," Mr. Linden said, "but I can't help but think why somebody would take it. I set one rule, and of course somebody had the need to break it."

Jamie's heart pounded in her chest. Her face turned as red as a tomato, and her ears burned like fire. Jamie didn't know what to do next. Should she tell Mr. Linden the truth? Or should she just play along and say it was somebody else? She felt awkward standing there so suspiciously, so she blurted out something she immediately regretted.

"Um, Mr. Linden? When I was leaving yesterday, outside the library I saw a girl holding *The Secret Garden* book that had your library sticker on the back of it."

She trembled with every word she said.

"What did she look like?" Mr. Linden asked.

"Uh, she looked younger than me, and she was thin and scraggly. She also had blond hair."

Jamie tried to look as calm as Mr. Linden always did, but inside she was freaking out! She had just described Mary, the main character in *The Secret Garden*! She couldn't believe it; how could she be so stupid? Mr. Linden would know she was lying right away! After all, he was the one who had recommended the book in the first place. So he had probably read it.

Jamie didn't know what to do next, so she picked up her backpack and hurriedly said good-bye to Mr. Linden.

"Oh, and remember to look out for that thief," Mr. Linden called on to Jamie as she pushed open the door.

"Will do, Mr. Linden," Jamie replied, her voice still a little bit shaky.

Jamie was so worked up with the incident that she didn't

open her closet for a whole week, and eventually she forgot about the whole fiasco. When Jamie opened her closet later to get her secret stash of candy, she almost fainted. The vines were everywhere.

The vines had wrapped around the rest of her closet and the candy jar. Jamie came to her senses. She realized that she had to tell Mr. Linden the truth, or her problem would just get worse. Jamie quickly closed the closet door, grabbed her coat, and ran out the door to the library.

"Mr. Linden," she said. "I took *The Secret Garden* book, and now there are vines growing everywhere in my apartment. I am so sorry."

With that, Jamie burst into tears. Mr. Linden stood up and walked over to Jamie. He put his gentle hand on Jamie's shoulder.

"Thank you for telling me the truth. I knew this would happen. I wanted to tell you when I saw you taking the book, but I figured you should learn a lesson."

"Can you help me?" Jamie asked, trembling.

"Hmm, I think everyone deserves a second chance."

Together Mr. Linden and Jamie raced to her apartment. When they got to her apartment room, Jamie saw that the vines had grown everywhere and had wrapped all over her bed. The vines were growing faster than ever, swirling in every direction. Luckily Mr. Linden had brought along his long Spanish sword.

He jumped and twirled, slid and ducked, slashing the vines everywhere. Finally Mr. Linden could open Jamie's closet. He pulled the roots from the glowing center of the book. There was a lot of pulling to be done. Jamie, who had less gracefully made it to the closet, helped in pulling, too.

Finally the roots flew out, and the surrounding vines all shriveled up. Mr. Linden stuffed the whole green mess back into the book.

Together they walked back to the library, ensuring that the book was kept closed.

Now that Jamie had learned her lesson, she had become Mr. Linden's trusted library helper.

Jamie helped Mr. Linden reorganize the library so that all the magical books were in one section. Jamie and some of her new best friends from book club at school formed their own secret library club. They were the only kids in Jacksonville who knew about the mysterious magical books in Mr. Linden's library.

Scorpion on the Rock

Niharika Thuppanna

(Age: Ten)

*I*t was a hot and sweaty morning in India. Raju woke up to the sounds of pots and pans. As he walked into the kitchen sleepily, he saw his grandmother struggling to lift a gigantic water pot.

"Let me hold it, *Ajji* [Grandma]," he said as he shifted the pot into his hand. The weight of the pot numbed his hands. Raju was at his grandparent's house over the summer, when he got a break from his school.

"Raju, can you please take this pot to the well and bring fresh water back to me?" asked his grandmother. The well was four blocks away.

Raju groaned but answered, "Yes, *Ajji*."

Raju ran into the tiny bathroom and started brushing his teeth with the water left from the previous day's collection. He then washed his hands and brushed his hair with a small comb and wondered why the comb always had a few missing sticks. Then he ran back into the kitchen and took the pot from his struggling grandmother.

He pushed the small wooden door and waved good-bye to his loving grandmother. *Moo. Baa. Woof, woof.* Those were the sounds Raju had to deal with every summer morning on his grandfather's farm. Of course, it was a farm, so one should expect those sorts of sounds people used to communicate with the animals.

A Window to Young Minds

When Grandmother said, "Go fetch water from the well," she usually meant five trips to the well.

When Raju was coming back from his fourth trip, he saw that his cousin was playing with the neighborhood boys. Raju looked around a few times. He had a mischievous idea that he would go play with the boys and finish his fifth round later. But what would he tell his grandmother? She would probably be angry with him! That's when it hit him. He would tell his grandmother that he had tripped over a sharp rock and it had hurt so badly that he had sat there crying for hours. He dropped the pot and ran off to play with the boys. In his excitement, he didn't realize he had broken the pot.

Raju was now living the life! It was monsoon season, and rain slowly picked up as Raju played with his friends. He was far away from home. They played with the lazy cows standing in the shade of a small neem tree. They played marbles in the rain, ate mangoes, and even fed a stray dog.

Time passed faster than usual, and it was getting late. Raju decided to go back home right away. But then he noticed that his feet and hands were covered in dirt and mud.

How come they smell so bad? Raju thought to himself. Then Raju realized his feet were covered in cow dung. Raju hovered over to a puddle in disgust.

He looked for a rock to kneel on, because the outside of the puddle was covered in mud. Raju put one foot on a small rock he found and waded the other foot in the muddy water. He heard a strange noise near the small rock—but before he could understand, he felt a burning pinch on his right ankle.

"*Ouch!*" Raju yelled as tears flew down his cheeks. He looked around himself in pain and was relieved that there was no snake. Soon he was shocked to see a mad scorpion glaring at him. Raju leaped off the rock just to realize the small rock he was sitting on was the scorpion's property.

One part of little Raju was coping with the pain, but the other part was thinking what to do. Then his survival instincts kicked in. He knew it was time to start running, running to the village. All his little cousins and friends were running around him in disbelief. Raju wasn't running swiftly. He was actually limping.

Very quickly he realized that he might not make it to the village on his own in time.

"Hey, Sachin!" he yelled to one of his younger cousins. "Please go to the village and get some help."

But Sachin continued to run slowly right in front of little Raju and just kept staring.

"Go, go, go!" Raju yelled.

This made Sachin run a lot faster. Now Raju was running in the fields. Raju remembered the incident on the previous day when his sister had got bitten by a scorpion while sleeping outside under the stars. And he had thought that he would never get bitten by a scorpion. He had actually told that to someone.

The path was very narrow, with long grass on both sides waving in the cool breeze. It was impossible to see past the long grass. Raju had not noticed earlier that he was going slower and slower by the minute. Luckily the help arrived.

"Raju!" yelled Rohit, his older cousin who was working in the fields. Rohit had a plan, and without wasting a second, he went straight into action. He took his waistband off and tied it around Raju's affected calf in order to prevent the poison from spreading further.

They started running to the village again. After a few minutes, they reached the village, and more people began to find out about Raju's scorpion bite.

At home now, Raju was in a dreamlike state, surrounded by people. He heard whispers like, "He is not going to make it!" and "A scorpion from the wild? That is dangerous!" and "He will start feeling very cold."

In the beginning, Raju tried not to believe what the villagers said, but as he started to feel cold even though it was muggy outside, he started to believe them.

Instead of bringing him to the hospital, his mom, grandmother, and grandfather gave him homemade medicine. That was a *big* mistake, for it did not help little Raju at all, and Raju was getting colder by the minute.

They realized it soon and took poor little Raju to the government hospital in Dharmapura, the only nearby town with a hospital. His mother couldn't ride the bicycle he was carried on, so she ran beside it.

The hospital was a tiny structure in the shade of a big banyan tree. The inside walls were yellow with spider webs on the ceiling. They were lucky that there was a doctor in the hospital that day. During the previous summer, Raju had hurt his head, and when they had reached this hospital, they had found no doctor at work.

As soon the doctor came, he asked a few nonstop questions. "Where did it bite you? What kind of pain was it? Are you sure it was a scorpion?"

Without waiting to hear the answers of all his questions, the doctor rummaged through his small cabinets. The shelves were lined up with colorful liquids in bottles with small labels on them. Raju tried hard to put his focus back on the doctor. The doctor pulled out a syringe out of a container of boiling water. Then he filled the syringe with the yellow medicine in one of the small bottles. He asked Raju to turn on his stomach, lowered his shorts, and gave him a shot.

Short Stories by Young Writers

Raju continued to freeze. The doctor asked him to rest on a mat and covered him in three thick blankets.

Soon Raju was shivering so much that he completely lost consciousness. As soon as his mother found out, she started praying. His grandparents started looking for a way to take them to the county hospital thirty-three kilometers away in the city of Hiriyur.

They were lucky again to have found a car to take them to the county hospital. Raju's grandfather had been out arranging for it. He came inside the building and was ready to take Raju into the car.

But suddenly Raju opened his eyes.

"I am OK, *Tatha* [Grandpa]," Raju said to his grandfather who was staring at him in disbelief. In few minutes, Raju was walking again.

Soon Raju and his family left the hospital. They reached home safely and happily. Everyone had so many questions for Raju. But his grandmother just had one question.

"What did you do to that gigantic pot of mine?"

A Medicine of Love

Hannah Won

(Age: Fourteen)

*I*t was a gloomy night with the sky painted gray. The wind whistled harshly in the dark night. The raindrops fell heavily on the old family car of the Smith family as they were driving down the rough roads of Elmer's Street. After a long thirty-minute drive, Mr. and Mrs. Smith arrived at the front door of an orphanage.

The two stepped out of their car, and with beating hearts, they walked toward the building. With shaking hands Mrs. Smith grasped the door handle and pulled it open; it was going to be a new beginning for the Smith family.

Mrs. and Mr. Smith quickly met an assistant and were brought to a small room with a wooden table in the center.

Breaking the silence, the assistant said with a rather calm and bright voice, "Welcome, Mr. and Mrs. Smith. My name is Sarah Walls, and I will be your assistant in the process of becoming a foster parent. The boy you will be seeing today will be here in a couple minutes."

"Appreciate your help. Thank you!" Mrs. Smith said in a shaking tone.

Every tick of the second hand of the clock brought odd fear and nervousness to the new foster parents. Hardly a minute or two later, the door opened slightly, and the boy entered into the room. Mrs. Smith and Mr. Smith stared at the boy with a mixed emotion of sympathy and shock, for the

Short Stories by Young Writers

boy was wheeled in. He only had one leg, the right one. He rolled his wheelchair in, looked at the Smiths, and acted as if he did not see the shocked expressions.

"This is Ryan Brown. He is nine years old and quite honestly has not been in this orphanage for long. He's been here for about three weeks," Sarah said while itching her head, as though trying to remember the exact duration.

The four sat, and as Sarah nudged Ryan, he spoke.

"Hi, I'm Ryan, and it's OK if you don't adopt me because of my leg," he said dispiritedly.

Surprised at Ryan's words, Sarah quickly chuckled nervously and responded, "Ryan, dear, it's not like that. Please don't be rude to yourself."

Mrs. Smith peered at the boy. She saw his emotionless face and thought his words seemed ruthless and inconsiderate to say in front of someone who could possibly become his new parent. However, when she looked into his eyes, she knew almost immediately that there was something behind his deep blue eyes.

"Mrs. Smith, you have met all the requirements in adoption, and you wished the child for a boy. It's a matter of time when you want to take your child home. The forms are ready," Sarah said calmly.

Mr. Smith responded, "Whatever works the best for your orphanage. Like we discussed with you, we have decided to adopt any child irrespective of the circumstances."

"We'll adopt him," Mrs. Smith said with a bit of an unsure tone.

The two, now foster parents, filled out forms and signed their names. Once in a while, Mrs. Smith looked up at the boy, and she promised herself that she would make him happy no matter what.

A Window to Young Minds

After a heavy load of paper work, Mr. and Mrs. Smith rolled Ryan to their car. There was unbreakable awkwardness in the air. Mrs. Smith had thought that when an orphan was adopted, the child would scream and cry in happiness, but this boy almost seemed like he was sad.

As Mr. Smith started driving, the Smiths asked a few basic questions. The responses were curt and simple. A thirty-minute drive seemed longer than the one earlier in the day when they had driven to the orphanage.

Mrs. Smith confidently opened the door and yelled, "Andrew! Come down! Your new brother is here! Come on, come down!"

In response to the calling, Andrew hurried down the stairs and saw the boy. As soon as he saw Ryan, Andrew peered down and saw his missing leg.

"Mom, who told you to bring a brother home like that? Who even told you to bring home a brother?" Andrew screamed.

"Andrew Smith! Watch out for your attitude!" Mrs. Smith yelled back.

"Please, Andrew, let's not be rude," Mr. Smith remarked.

Ryan roamed his eyes to the ground and was speechless.

"Follow me right now to your room," Mrs. Smith demanded to Andrew.

With angered faces, Mrs. Smith and Andrew stomped into a room. Mrs. Smith locked the room behind her.

"Andrew, who do you think you are to talk like that in front of your new brother!" Mrs. Smith hollered.

Andrew shot back, "He's not my brother! You think a boy like that could replace Matthew? You think that you can put any boy in front of me, and I will joyfully accept him as my brother? Mom, it hasn't even been a year since Matthew died!

How could you be so forgetful! He was my real brother, and I don't need anyone else!"

Shocked, Mrs. Smith looked at Andrew and claimed, "I never said I was replacing Matthew. Matthew's loss is as much a terrifying memory to me as he is to you! I'm doing this to help you!"

Mrs. Smith marched out the door and rushed downstairs.

"Well, who said I needed your help?" Andrew mumbled under his breath.

"Sorry about that, Ryan. It's not your fault. Don't worry," Mrs. Smith apologized.

Mr. Smith and Mrs. Smith helped Ryan set up his room and quickly tucked him in bed. Tears welled up in Mrs. Smith eyes as she left the room.

As Mrs. Smith and Mr. Smith hit their bed, Mr. Smith exclaimed, "Honey, I know it's hard. We knew it would be hard from the beginning. Everything takes time; time will heal things."

Mrs. Smith sobbed, "I'm not too sure now if this is the right decision. If I think of Matthew, I feel like I'm doing the worst thing, but if I think of Andrew, I feel like this is the only thing that will help him."

Mr. Smith comforted, "Sweetheart, Matthew suffered from leukemia, but even in those times, he looked to Andrew and laughed through his pain. I'm sure if Andrew becomes happy, Matthew will also be laughing and smiling in heaven."

The next day the sun shone bright through the windows in the house. It was like any other day. Mrs. Smith was preparing breakfast, and Mr. Smith was reading the newspaper, drinking a cup of coffee. Ryan wheeled into the kitchen from his room and sat quietly in his wheelchair.

A few moments later, Andrew stepped downstairs, and the

family had breakfast quietly. Mrs. Smith looked up once in a while to look at the two boys. As soon as Andrew finished his last slice of bacon, he put his spoon down and stomped back upstairs.

"I'm sorry for this awkwardness; it's not what he truly intends. He is still dealing with the loss of his brother." Mrs. Smith sighed, looking at Ryan.

"It's OK, I guess. I'm used to this kind of stuff," Ryan said as he rolled himself to his room.

Days passed by, and neither Ryan nor Andrew showed any signs of opening his heart to the other. Mr. and Mrs. Smith even contemplated returning Ryan to the orphanage for the good of the boys.

On a sunny morning about two weeks later, after finishing their breakfast, Andrew sat at the couch to watch TV, and Ryan rolled back to his room. Andrew noticed the headline in the newspaper kept at the table in front of him. *A Terrifying Incident*, it read in dark bold letters at the top of the front page. Curious, Andrew read a few lines and then came across a picture, a picture very familiar. It was Ryan. He was standing in front of a basketball court, smiling. The newspaper read,

> *On June fifth, nine-year-old Ryan Brown (leftmost in the picture), champion of the national junior basketball competition, faced tragedy after his win. A horrific car accident killed thirty-six-year-old Matt Brown and thirty-four-year-old Kayla Brown. It has been reported that the accident has caused champion Ryan Brown to have his left leg amputated.*

Traumatized, bursting with sympathy, Andrew had tears swirled in his eyes. He couldn't believe what he had just read.

Short Stories by Young Writers

He suddenly realized all his selfishness and his unwillingness to look into the sadness Ryan would have been carrying. Andrew was now lost in the memories of when his little brother, Matthew, would throw the basketball into the air and he would catch it and shoot it in. He had bonded with his little brother through their common love of sports. He now became conscious of the pain Ryan would have been going through by losing his parents and his ability to play the sport.

"What have I been doing?" Ryan sniffed.

He realized that he shared a similarity with Ryan, a tragic loss. They both needed someone to fill in the emptiness caused by the loss of a loved one with the medicine of love.

Andrew stood up and ran to Ryan's room. He slowly opened the door and peered in.

With excitement, Andrew spoke. "Hey! Wanna play a game of basketball?"

Mr. Schaeffer's Trench Coat

Tarisha Badaya

(Age: Fourteen)

People tend to take the things around them for granted or completely ignore them. Some people do observe; some people do get curious, but they truly understand the importance or learn a lesson only after those things are gone.

I realized this even better after Mr. Schaeffer disappeared during fall 2002, when I was only seven years old. Everyone in the neighborhood recognized him as the eccentric old man who almost always wore a dark-gray trench coat with matching pants, a white shirt, a black tie, formal shoes that always seemed to be polished, and a beret.

The beret, however, was a piece of clothing that I thought was not as unusual as the rest of his secretive attire; after all, his family was from France. Papa told me about how his family had managed to escape from France during the spread of the Holocaust around the late 1930s. No one else really seemed to care as much as I did, since everyone seemed to only pay attention to Mrs. Osborn's stories about her frequent visits to New York City to visit her children.

Life was very ordinary in our neighborhood in Poughkeepsie, New York. The teenagers were busy in their teenager-like activities—to which I was completely oblivious at the time, since even my elder brother, Jeff, was only ten at the time. I did however, go out to the playground every evening around five o'clock with Jeff and found a number of kids my age and younger playing, shadowed by the deciduous trees, in a weather that was never too warm. And every day I noticed Mr. Schaeffer walk past the park, down the lane, and into his old house, which stood out; the peeling paint and the gloomy feeling around his house didn't drive many visitors, making him the pariah of the neighborhood.

But I knew he wasn't all that lonely. This dawned upon me when one day he did not promenade down our lane at the usual time, which made me quickly sneak out past my brother's peripheral vision, outside the park and no farther. That's where I saw him turning into our lane and putting what seemed to be an old DSLR camera inside a large pocket of his gray trench coat.

The following night while I was having a qualm that I had definitely forgotten something for school, my mind went off on a tangent, and I found myself wondering why I had never previously noticed Mr. Schaeffer carrying a camera although I had seen him carrying grocery bags before.

Papa always told me that I was an inquisitive child. Even though my father always appeared to have a profusion of knowledge about almost everything and everyone I could think of, he was quiet until Jeff or I asked him a question. Mom was the creative one in our family. Her love for cooking was almost as strong as her love for our family.

Several typical summer days went by. After our exams were over, Jeff and I had enough time to watch TV, play the few video games we had, read books, and go out in the park, where we only saw younger children and their parents. Some adults seemed to get along, while others sat on the benches and watched their children cavort in the playground.

Toward the end of summer, things started to change a bit. Not in the run-of-the-mill lifestyle of the people of our neighborhood but in the clothing, style, and overall attitude of the old man. For two weeks in a row, I saw him walking without his trench coat, which was ironic because it was getting colder. Strangely he also did not have the unusually restful countenance on his face. Instead what I could see was a slightly languishing soul. Every time I saw him those days, I had a queasy feeling in my stomach, as if I were riding a roller coaster not meant for me.

I remembered the times when he had turned around and looked toward the park almost every day all those years. I had then started smiling back at him every time he looked. I knew he smiled back at me, because I could see the wrinkles around his small gray eyes start to appear deeper, his small lips widen, and his cheekbones slightly rise.

A few days later, Mr. Schaeffer was walking down the lane with a plastic bag, and as I looked toward him, I saw his fingers twitching and the bag falling down on the street, while Mr. Schaeffer stared at the white bag. I felt my legs running toward him as Jeff followed me. I stood in front of Mr. Schaeffer under the shadow of the colorful trees, picked up the bag—which seemed very light and flimsy—for him, and gently handed it to him.

I finally opened my mouth and said, "Hi, Mr. Schaeffer," in a voice that Jeff told me sounded very warm and sweet the following night when we went over this, making me feel satisfied.

He replied by saying, "Why, good evening, Miss Nancy."

His voice was soft and calming, which made it feel like someone had unlocked an old treasure chest. This feeling was also reassured by Jeff, since we were shocked that he even knew my name. He started walking to his house, and I felt the urge to speak something; hence, I opened my mouth and quickly said, "See you tomorrow," while waving my arm.

He looked back. But this time I was unable to recognize his expression. Glad that I had finally seen the old man closely and talked to him, I returned to Jeff, who was waiting for me near the park fence. We then walked home. Unfortunately Mr. Schaeffer didn't come outside after that; he disappeared, leaving behind an enigma that I did not welcome or enjoy.

A thought often comes to my mind—that I had a chance to stop him from disappearing. One Sunday morning the air felt different when I woke up. I walked out of the house and intuitively looked to my right and saw the door to Mr. Schaeffer's house open. There were neon-yellow plastic strips wrapped around his house's porch, which my seven-year-old mind knew meant to not enter.

But being the inquisitive and rebellious person I am, particularly because I hadn't seen him for few days, I looked to make sure nobody was watching and ran into his house. I quietly walked on his porch, stepped on the threshold, and then walked into his house. Every step was like a drop of water dripping from a stalactite into the small puddles of water in an empty cave. But as I entered the house, I was startled.

The roller coaster had now dropped from the highest point, and it was a thrilling relief. On top of the mantel, I saw beautiful black and white and colored framed photographs of people, people who were young in some pictures and were older in others. A familiar-looking young and wonderful man in the pictures caught my eye, and I smiled wide as I realized that Mr. Schaeffer had a better sense of clothing when he was younger. I still funnily remember being amazed when I saw his big family, including his beautiful wife, in those pictures.

A Window to Young Minds

Now when I look back and think about him, I understand his life better. I advanced into the house, and my bewilderment turned into a slight, pleasurable excitement.

The hallways were decorated with aesthetic photographs of nature and the environment. I recall seeing pictures of the Hudson River, the streets, flora and fauna, and busy strangers walking and working. Even as a child, I understood that such photographs required not only skill but also passion and love. After mentally capturing these photographs and looking at the background and foreground of each, while my eyes were wide open, I slowly entered the only bedroom that was open. It was a cache of memories, just like his entire home.

A second after I entered the room, I was thrilled to see a huge canvas, on which there was a painting that got printed on my mind forever. It was a marvelous oil painting that consisted of me, Jeff, the children in the playground, their parents, and the park.

Next to the large canvas was another one of his developed photographs, which was the original copy from which the picture was painted clipped to a string. Down on the windowsill and on top of the cabinet, I saw a collection of natural and artificial paintbrushes of different sizes, which still had remains of paint on them. It was captivating. It was beautiful.

I realized, and still wonder about today, that all of these events took place while Mrs. Osborn had her weekly get-togethers, teenagers were busy doing their usual teenage stuff, and Jeff and I played in the park.

The little things inside the big picture mattered. I still find myself thinking that despite the dim lighting in that house that day, Mr. Schaeffer's home was illuminated by that painting, those photographs, those memories, those stories, and even those things that went unnoticed. I decided not to enter the other two locked rooms in order to respect his privacy and left.

At times I regret leaving on that day without looking for him. It seemed like the only chance to stop him from disappearing. But then life isn't about regretting the past, Papa says.

Meadow's Tale

Kydn Aurora Meyer

(Age: Ten)

Meadow, a white-bellied, ginger she-cat, appeared carrying a small, mouselike rodent in her jaws. She gazed for a moment at the small clearing that she had lived in for the past two years of her life. She spotted the small clump of sage bushes, which she had recently turned into a fairly decent den. The cat shrugged, trotted into the clearing, and lay down to eat her newly caught vole.

"Hello?" she said, her head snapping up as she heard a soft rustling in her den. She approached it gingerly, every step more cautious than the last. She was less than a tail-length away from her den, her fur bristling with nervousness, as she saw a pair of beady blue eyes stare at her.

"Who are you?" screeched Meadow, her claws digging into the ground. A few moments later, a pearly white she-cat hopped out of the bush. Meadow took a small step back as the cat turned to her with a warm grin on her face.

"Hello!" said the new cat. "I'm Marble!"

Meadow took another step back, trying to think of something to say.

"You're Meadow, right?" mewed Marble bubbly.

Meadow sighed and thought for a moment about what to say before responding simply, "Yeah." She heard a contented purr ripple through Marble's throat before fading into a low grumble.

"Good!" Marble said. "We'd better be going if we're going to make it in time for Moon Meal."

Meadow's fur bristled again as she thought briefly of that odd term, *Moon Meal*, and wondered what it meant.

Trying to remain calm, Meadow shrugged it off and looked at Marble. "Why should I come with you?" she finally said.

"I told Ember I should be able to tell you more," Marble mumbled more to herself than to Meadow. "Just trust me, OK?"

Meadow stopped thinking about what could happen and sighed. "Fine," she said briskly. "I'll come, but one wrong move…"

Marble seemed to get the point. She padded off, glancing back at her, as Meadow followed a few tail-lengths behind. As she looked at the thick forest around them, she realized that Marble was taking her through a path of the woods that, from what she could tell, not a single cat had passed through.

"Hey, Marble," she mewed. "This seems like an oddly dense bit of forest."

Meadow began to worry, thinking that possibly this could all have been a trap or an ambush, but Marble just laughed and looked back at her.

"I go through this side of the forest all the time!" Marble said, her bright blue eyes boring into Meadow's deep hazel ones. Meadow somehow felt safer with this cat than alone.

It had been at least a few hours by now, and Meadow's paw pads were beginning to ache as faint bits of bright orange, yellow, and subtle but stunning shades of pink appeared in the sky. She gazed up at the entrancing sky and ran right into Marble as she suddenly stopped. Meadow composed herself and noticed that there was an odd clump of ferns in front of them.

"Torrent!" meowed Marble, and to Meadow's surprise, a handsome, slender gray tomcat with deep brown pools for eyes, which seemed to go on forever, appeared out of the thick brush.

"Marble!" said Torrent, giving her a light nuzzle before turning to Meadow. "And you are?"

She jumped, and a warm feeling spread through the tips of her paws up to the edge of her nose.

"I'm Meadow," she chirped in a sheepish tone.

Torrent smiled and said, "Well, you're just in time for Moon Meal!"

Again the odd term flowed through her brain before disappearing as Meadow followed Torrent and Marble to a grassy hill. As she reached the top, she could see a small valley splattered with miniscule mounds. She could see a few cats as well, but then she spotted it: a beautiful, stunning oak tree with spiraling branches and bright green leaves. She realized very suddenly that this was not just an ordinary valley full of mounds. It was a camp.

"It's wonderful," Meadow whispered at a loss for words.

"Isn't it?" said Torrent, making her jump. He gave her a slight smirk and beckoned her forward. "Let's go," he said. "It's time for the Moon Meal."

She followed down the hill and reached the farthest mound from the main tree. There she found a new cat. He was short-haired and had black patches of fur on his stark, white pelt and soft amber eyes with a tired gleam in them.

"Who is he?" Meadow asked Torrent. Watching the cat, she noticed his thin visible ribs.

"We call him Patch," mewed Torrent. "Though his real name is Yarrow."

They finally got to the camp center after Torrent introduced her to a few other cats. Most of them were elders, but some were Bottom Cats from the outer edges, like Violet and Stitch, who were two bottom-rank siblings. Meadow sat down and saw Torrent move away from her to another cat, a russet-colored she-cat with ivy green eyes.

"A warm welcome to all the cats of the Clutter of Valleys," said the russet she-cat to the group. "And a special welcome to the new cat today."

Meadow jumped as the cat's gaze settled on her. She curled her tail around herself defensively.

"Meadow," said the she-cat. "Please step up."

Meadow trotted up, her ears shooting back as she felt the eyes of so many cats landing on her.

"I am Ember," the she-cat meowed as Meadow came nose to nose with her. "Welcome to the Clutter."

Meadow forced herself not to step back when Ember touched her nose. Suddenly she heard the sound of loud yowling rise up around her. She glanced at all the cats of the Clutter with their muzzles raised and their ears back, and Meadow began to yowl as well.

The noise began to fade, and she stopped to look around at the other cats. A few of them quieted or lowered their voices until all of the yowls were gone and they were all looking at Ember. She gave her Clutter a contented nod. Torrent stepped up and began to call the names of some of the other cats.

"Violet and Stitch," he called to the Bottom Cats. "Get the prey."

Meadow saw the thin, bony siblings trotting off to the largest mound and then trot back with a few mice, a skinny hare, and a small robin. She saw Ember go up and choose a mouse and step back with her share of the prey. After that, Torrent stepped up and took half of another mouse, leaving the rest for the other cats.

By the time it was Meadow's turn to eat, the mice were gone, and so was half of the hare. She glanced at the hare for a moment but padded up and took the robin instead, leaving the rest for the Bottom Cats to share the hare. She watched them fight over the rest of the prey and could see why the rest of the Clutter looked so malnourished.

Meadow watched the cats disperse and head to their designated mounds.

"Over here," said Torrent, and a warm feeling spread across her cheeks. He walked her over to a mound near a tree. She lay down in its shadow and fell asleep almost instantly.

She awoke from a prod from Marble and looked lazily up at the pearly white she-cat with annoyance.

"Wake up!" Marble mewed, and Meadow got to her feet carefully. "You're coming on patrol with me today!"

Marble began to walk away with Meadow following her as they circled the mounds farthest from the tree before turning away facing the forest.

"Scope out the rocks and bushes," Marble mewed. "Anywhere cats or Red Paws could hide."

Meadow nodded but asked, "Red Paws? You mean foxes?"

Marble gave her a quick nod, and they continued the patrol silently.

They began to climb over the largest hill across from the forest, and Meadow thought there was nothing worth checking. Then they got to the top. She spotted small silhouettes of some sort of a pack or herd.

"It's probably a herd of Long Hooves," Marble said dismissively, but Meadow felt her fur prickle oddly.

"I'd better tell Ember anyway," Meadow mewed, starting to trot back. "Keep patrolling without me!" she added.

Meadow looked around the camp and saw Torrent, Yarrow, and another cat she hadn't met. They were preparing to leave for hunting. She saw Torrent nod, and the group left. Once they were gone, she turned to the large oak and noticed that it had a small hollow at the base just large enough for a cat to fit in. She squeezed through the gap and saw Ember sitting down on a dirt mound that looked almost like a throne.

"Ember," Meadow said, giving her leader a respectful nod. "Marble and I spotted something that seemed like herd of…" She hesitated for a moment before saying, "Long Hooves."

Ember had barely nodded before they heard a blood-curdling scream. Meadow froze as she realized it was Marble. She rushed out behind Ember to see Marble fighting what seemed to be at least five wolves.

"Large Paw attack!" called Ember to the Clutter. "Violet! Stitch! Help Marble get back to Leader's Oak!" The two sprinted at the Large Paws, viciously tackling the one that had attacked Marble.

Meadow gasped and looked at Marble as she ran to the tree.

"Marble!" she cried. "Your eye!"

Marble's eye was closed, but one could see the blood

staining her perfect white fur. Meadow nuzzled her carefully and let her run into the hollow, leaving a steady trail of blood behind her.

A blur of russet fur flashed Meadow's vision, and she saw Ember dive at one of the wolves' throat. The wolf shook his large shaggy head, tossing her off, but she landed swiftly on her feet and then dived back, a furious gleam in her eyes. Meadow turned away from Ember just in time to see Stitch fall, scarlet blood flowing from his neck. Meadow gasped, and as the wolf turned to help his friend kill Violet, she approached Stitch, still and lifeless. She looked at the gray tabby, his amber eyes stuck open, and then looked at Violet, who looked almost exactly like her brother except for her mossy green eyes.

"Watch out!" Meadow mewed to Violet as the wolf that had killed Stitch lunged at her. Violet dodged and caught site of Stitch.

"Stitch!" she screamed, sprinting to her brother. Meadow guarded her as she tried in vain to wake her brother.

"To Leader's Oak!" Meadow called, leading the remaining survivors to the tree just as a wolf snapped at her throat. The wolves snarled and tried to stick their muzzles through the hollow before they padded away.

"W-why are they leaving?" said a shaky Violet.

Meadow screamed, "Ember is still out there!"

The whole Clutter froze as they could only wait to see what would remain of their noble leader.

A few minutes afterward, the valley went silent. Meadow stepped out and gasped, speechless. She looked at her leader's body, ragged and almost unrecognizable. Cats came out all around her, sat down in a mass, and mourned. Meadow began to yowl and was followed by Violet. Slowly the remainder of the Clutter was yowling, honoring the fallen cats.

After the Clutter went silent once more, they were joined by the hunting party.

Violet spoke up. "We need a new leader," she mewed. "And I, for one, think it should be Meadow. She guarded me when Stitch died."

Many of the cats nodded. A few of the cats objected.

Torrent came to the front to help.

"Though Meadow acted bravely, she has only been with us for a day," he said.

Meadow looked at Torrent and those deep brown eyes.

"We will have a leader's vote," said Torrent. "Whosoever is chosen will train Meadow to be the successor."

Meadow stepped up. "I agree with Torrent," she said. "I want to help, but I'm not ready to be a leader.

"At least not right now," she added. She wanted to try and help the cats she had grown so fond of. She thought back over her years of loneliness. Her mother had died when she was a kitten, followed by her entire family. She had spent years surviving on her own fortitude.

Meadow realized she had found something she had lost a long time ago: a family.

A Window to Young Minds

Breaking Through

Ankita S. Karuturi

(Age: Ten)

My lungs feel like they are ripping in two. I cannot run anymore, but I have an eerie feeling, like something or someone is behind me. I slow down, looking around at the half-lit signs of the street, which was once probably bustling with people shopping, eating, dancing. Now it is silent, except for me. Then I feel it again. This presence. This thing.

I spin around, trying to catch it. Again nothing. I stagger backward, unsure if this is a safe place for me to be. I turn to run down the alley when I run into someone. For a second, we are a tangled confusion. Slowly we separate.

"Rosie!" I gasp.

A look of relief flashes on her face. "Poppy!" Rosie yells in an angry tone that is all too familiar. Her face floods with anger. "I should have expected it…" Her voice trails off.

"Expected what?" I ask her.

"Nothing!" She snaps back to reality. I hear a hissing sound behind me, like something large is fast approaching.

"We've got to go!" Rosie yells. Her face turns pale.

"You can hear it, too?" I ask.

"Yeah," she says. "Of course I can."

She looks at me like I am crazy for asking. Finally the noise stops. We crouch next to a Dumpster near what was once a Quickie Mart.

"What was that back there?" I ask, still shaken after seeing Rosie.

"I'm not sure what that was," Rosie says innocently. "Maybe it was just the wind."

"Let's get out of here," I say. "It smells like rotten pizza. Come on!"

Rosie grabs my hand, taking me through alleys and streets I didn't know existed. Everything seems a little bit off. The roofs are uneven, colors are brighter, streams shimmer in the sun, flowers smell stronger and sweeter, and the lights seem to sparkle.

I think to myself, *This is the sight of freedom. No more fear of the unknown, no more worries...for a moment at least.* As long as we keep moving, I know we are safe. This place is a paradise.

Rosie moves with a purpose, but she evades any questions about what we are doing, why we are doing it, and what she knows that I don't.

We finally come to a house that seems too small for someone to live in. It has caramel-colored shutters and a roof with shingles that look like they are made of peanut brittle.

Rosie grabs my shoulders and says intensely, "Wait right here. Do not move. Do not talk to anyone. Do not answer anyone. *Wait here!*"

There is a fire of urgency in her eyes that scares away any questions I may have. I slump down on the front stoop as she slips into the house, and I realize how tired I am from walking and running.

Questions flood my mind.

Why is Rosie going in there? Is that even a house? If she wants to keep me safe, why can't I go inside? Why can't I talk to anyone? Wait, there is really no one to talk to. Now that I think of it, I haven't seen a single person since I ran into Rosie. Where is everyone? The streets are empty, but it is daytime. This is New York, right?

All of a sudden, the air shifts. A weight presses toward me, and I feel the air leave my lungs. It's here! It's here! I must run! Run! *Run!*

I break into a full sprint, as fast as my legs can carry me. I don't know where I am. I don't know where I am going. All I know is that I have to run.

I remember Rosie's words, nagging in the back of my mind. *Wait here.*

Why did she tell me not to move? She should have known better. But still...She had said it with so much force. She must have had *some* reason.

That doesn't matter now. I have to run.

Up ahead, I see the sliver of an old brick alley. There has to be something or someone there that can help me. Maybe I can hide in one of the stores. Stay calm. Breathe.

I turn into the alley. There is nothing there except for an old factory with double doors, crumbling bricks, broken windows, and a partly caved roof. Paint the color of mud is pealing from years of wear. Slivers of bright-white brick peak out, shadowed by dirt and moss. Carved into the wood of the door is an image of the sun. What could that mean? It seems kind of creepy, yet it has an odd familiarity to it.

This door is my only chance for escape. I push the brass handle, but it doesn't budge. I try the other handle, and it only rattles as I throw my weight against the sun carving.

I feel its weight crush me as it descends down the alley toward me. It hisses ominously, "Give me the necklace, and I will leave you."

My necklace? Why would anybody want my necklace? It

doesn't matter. It is the only thing I have left of my parents, and nobody is going to take it from me. I rip the necklace off my neck. The ground seems to shift as I pound and push on the old doors, trying to escape with my life.

I throw myself with all my might one last time at the doors, and the necklace laces my hand and begins to burn and light as if it is on fire. It bursts into a flash of light and consumes everything around me. The light dances on my back and gathers into the shape of wings. The weight of the presence that was chasing me seems to have disappeared. Stunned, I look at the wings that have emerged on my back. Am I a bird? Am I a butterfly? What were these wings? Were they mine?

They can't fly, can they? I need to keep running. But I am too tired to take another step. It might be back any moment, though. I need to get out of here! Suddenly the wings lift me off the ground. At first I am shaky and unsure. But then with a sense of purpose, I float over the factory. It is as if the wings can read my mind and are carrying me away. I stand on top of the factory. Its roof is a burnt mess, like it had been through a fire. I look back and can feel the presence surging forward, trying to push me to my death from my high perch above the building.

It is now or never to make my escape. "Please work," I pray. I jump off the building. I drop down, plummeting few feet before I rocket, spinning in a whirlwind of magical flight.

I fly away as fast as I can. I feel free for the first time. Sure, I am still being chased, but now I have the ability to run—no, *fly*—to safety. I am in control. I rocket through the air so fast I **can** outrun a cheetah. I mean out*fly* a cheetah. I look back for my necklace, my saving grace. It isn't there; all that is left is a slight burn imprint where it had burst from in my hand. I have a sinking feeling, a fear. Where can it be? I feel like I have lost my parents again. Is it still back at the factory door? I weigh the thought of going back to look for it, but it is too dangerous to return to the last place I encountered the presence.

I want to collapse right there in the middle of the New York City sky. I feel like a sparrow who has just been shot in the heart. I glide toward the streets of New York. I allow myself to return, grounded in the world I had thought I knew. What am I?

I walk, trying to clear my head and understand all the things that have just happened. I find myself searching for things that I know are true. The sun. The sun is real. The thought of the sun makes me miss everything: my parents, our old home, my necklace. I am on a street with rows of shops on my right and my left. Not many people are there, and if they see my wings, they don't let on. Maybe only I can see them. There is a lot still to sort out.

All of a sudden, I have a pit in my stomach, like I lost something. I know I have lost the necklace. That isn't it. What can it be? Then, like a bolt of lightning, it hits me.

Rosie!

Nature's Music

Christopher Joseph Maxwell

(Age: Sixteen)

When I held my first and only child, I envisioned my life etched onto his tiny body; at the age of twenty-four minutes, my son was already going to be a musician. A cellist. A prodigy who pushed ahead of his peers and made a life for himself. He would become the next great instrumentalist, and when I saw his eyes welded shut and his arms constantly searching for something to grasp, I knew he was born to become a musician. In this moment, he inherited my art and passion.

He cried in my arms. His first song. Truly a child's first cry is the sonority of nature, and we humans can never fully comprehend the complexity of nature's music. His wailing represented my aspirations for the baby.

I knew that it was wrong to impose a life upon a child.

The truth is that I loathed myself for being so selfish in making him become a musician, but my deepest desires prevailed. At the age of three, he had started singing, learning solfège, and developing his ear. By his grand age of four, he held a cello.

The first note he played was a G. He struck the open G string, and he produced a metallic, scraping sound. This new thing made him giggle. He struck the note again, and his smile made me feel profound feelings of love. I wanted to hold him in my arms, to embrace him.

He looked at me and searched for confirmation, and I nodded at him.

"Go on," I chirped. "You sound good."

My vocabulary was limited with him, but I loved speaking to the child. My son, Joseph Barnes, was quite the linguist.

By two he spoke, slipping and stuttering over the petite words his mind could muster. Things such as *Mama*, *Dada*, and *Baba* escaped his lips. When he was three, he could connect words and ask for different foods for which he yearned. He would stretch one chubby finger to the Honey Nut Cheerios.

"Mama, hungry, cereal."

Jane and I were so proud.

Joey took the bow again and cut at the A string. It resonated with a gritty texture, but it was a note. And my son actually loved playing it. This was his first venture into music, and I could hardly contain my deep joy.

"Daddy, I made that," he said, searching my eyes for signs of happiness.

"Yes, you did, Joey. And Daddy is proud of you. He loves your music so much."

I absorbed his giddy state and started laughing and smiling. Tears welled in my eyes as I showed him how to press down on the string.

He played a sharp E natural on the D string. Seeing my wide grin, Joseph replayed the note. Timidly he pressed four fingers down and played his first G, an octave higher than his first note on the cello. The pitch of this new G was flat enough to be an F sharp, but he was playing. All that mattered in the universe was sitting in front of me, beholding his first instrument. His sheepish approach to the cello made me love him more than anything.

It was then, through months of determined practice, that Joseph Barnes started to read music, and thereafter he could take those foreign words on the page—take all of the crescendos and diminuendos, take all of the scales and arpeggios—and craft something new with them.

I could scarcely believe what I was hearing. This child wasn't just fingering the notes that he saw; he actually produced something of his own. This was what I wanted all of my life.

At age five, he gathered an ascending line—D, E, F sharp, and G—and played through them, increasing volume as he perambulated up the tetrachord. He was only five, yet this complicated idea of musicality started surfacing in his mind!

At the age of eight, Joseph started his first concerto. The first Haydn piece. He received the music and placed it on his stand as I watched over his every move. At this point Joseph Barnes had learned all of the three octave scales and had launched himself into thumb position. His time had been consumed by score studying, practicing, listening to the masters such as Ma and Rostropovich, and contemplating his life as a musician.

Would he be a touring soloist or member of a symphony? Music had become his one great love, and his liking of everything else slowly dissipated. He looked at the piece of music and mentally prepared himself.

He started to sight-read. Playing the first thirty-second notes, he shifted with ease, and fluidly he continued on with the simple tune.

I furrowed my brow. My eyes poured over his skin, and I heard everything he did. My ears were so acute that I could hear each time he slid into fifth position or each time he took a deep breath in order to maintain the pulse. I observed everything, and I was immediately aware of any mistake he made. Under my watch, he would be perfect.

Each time I did this, I had a creeping suspicion that what I was doing would damage the child, yet I followed through with these actions. In my later years, after what transpired, I have realized that I didn't love Joe as much as I loved his talent.

Every mistake took a toll on Joseph Barnes. He bit his lip or swore under his breath. With each error, he would replay the line ten times over, ensuring that the error would never happen again. His persistence should have been disturbing to me; however, I ignored the warning signs. Instead of being concerned that an eight-year-old hated himself for missing a note or maybe two, something so insignificant, I beckoned him forward. He had to be perfect.

No. I wouldn't let my failure as a musician translate into Joey's life. I wasted so much time practicing though never cultivating the proper skills. Joseph represented the thing that that I never became. I was never good enough, and so he would, under my constant supervision, become a virtuoso.

For this, I pushed him. So incredibly hard.

By age ten, he had started reading the Elgar Cello Concerto. The piece could make even the purest virtuosos faint. Even still, Barnes handled it very well, and he learned the piece in a meager eleven months.

Everyone at his recital was shocked by his command of phrasing and technical skill. In that moment, I knew everything was perfect, yet Joseph Barnes Davis walked off the stage without a single bow.

This was when he changed. A wash of anger, fear, and

melancholy had doused over Barnes's whole mind. This was not how it was supposed to be. I began to hate him and everything he represented: failure, angst, and depression.

It started with small, vexing things. Things such as not practicing for a full four hours each day. Not really focusing during private instruction. The worst of it was his complete apathy for music and living in general.

My failure as a parent had been realized. I started yelling at him, not feeding him, and sometimes shaking and slapping him to ensure that he played cello.

Truly he was despondent. I would lecture him on the importance of taking music seriously.

"Yes, Dad," he would say, his voice absent of life.

His depression started at this point. He was never hungry. He scarcely played and even started failing easy classes.

This angered me. The shouting matches continued with new fervor. They would last all night as spittle escaped my lips and as my body shook with rage. The plates would vibrate, and the house would sink as my gargantuan voice thundered through the building. The planet itself shuddered with earthquakes each time my voice resonated.

Even so, Joseph Barnes did not move an inch. He would appease me and then make his move to bed. It was his own state of catatonia. His depression had fully consumed him.

And instead of helping him, I told him that he was the worst son I could have possibly had. As the tears stream down my face now, I pray for forgiveness, but I know that God never listens. I was the one who put a bow into my son's hands and, consequently, a piercing knife.

I hated my son but loved his music. Now as he remains under six feet of rock, dirt, and grass, his body is still and

A Window to Young Minds

quiet.

Nature's music has subsided, and forevermore, I am no father.

On the Prairie

Molly Heinold

(Age: Twelve)

"Stop moping, Christina," Stella said.

"It's hard not to mope when you have to move for the fourth time," ten-year-old Christina replied.

"Come on, it'll be an adventure!" Stella's twin sister, Minnie, said.

"I don't want to go on an adventure," Christina said and moved to the back of the wagon and sat down on a barrel.

"What's going on back there?" Mama asked from the seat at the front of the wagon.

"Christina's just moping and pouting," Stella said.

Christina spun around. "I am not pouting!"

"Stop it!" Mama said sternly.

Christina crossed her arms. She looked out the back of the wagon. The land was flat with tall grass and a few wildflowers. *Why do we have to move out here?* Christina thought. *All because of the Homestead Act.* The Homestead Act was where the government gave 160 acres of free land to anyone who was the head of a household. You had to pay a filing fee and live and farm the land for five years to keep it. *Wish I could be back home*, Christina thought.

"Whoa," Papa called, stopping the horses. "We're here!"

Christina quietly jumped out of the wagon. There before her stood two sod buildings, one on the left and one on the right. Behind the buildings, there were a well and a privy, which Christina could just faintly see. Christina stood there and looked at the area, her mouth hanging open in shock.

"That's the house," Papa said, pointing to the sod building to the right. Christina still stood there, staring.

"Hey, at least Papa came out here earlier to build our farm," Minnie said, trying to cheer Christina up.

"If he hadn't, we would be sleeping on the bare ground with only the bugs and wolves for company!" Stella said laughing.

"That's not funny!" Christina sulked.

"Don't just stand there with your mouth hanging open. Come help us!" Mama said. Christina helped her parents and sisters unpack the wagon and put the stuff in the house.

That night for dinner it was just buttered bread and boiled potatoes. Christina slept on a pallet on the floor that night with her head resting on a pillow and a patchwork quilt over her. Her parents slept on the bed, and her sisters slept on the trundle bed.

The next morning Christina woke up shivering from cold. She sat up. Christina smelled bacon and coffee. She looked around the room. Mama was by the stove cooking breakfast, and her sisters were still sleeping in the trundle bed.

"Whyyy's it ssoooo cccold?" Christina asked her mother, with her teeth chattering.

"It's snowing, and it has been all night," Mama replied. "Now please get dressed."

Christina got dressed and wrapped herself in the patchwork quilt that lay on her bed. As she sat down at the table, her sisters were getting up. Both of them were shivering like Christina still was. Mama put a plate of biscuits and bacon and a cup of milk in front of Christina. Christina had just taken a bite of biscuit when the front door opened, and in came Papa covered in snow. He looked like a walking snowman! Christina giggled.

Christina did chores after breakfast. After chores she went and sat on the bed where Mama was mending clothes. The room was loud with the howling of the wind. Minnie was looking out the window deep in thought. Stella was sitting on the trundle bed drawing in the notebook with the pencil her best friend had given her. Papa sat at the kitchen table cleaning his rifle. The only sound in the room was the howling of the wind.

"Are you here to help me mend?" Mama shouted to Christina.

"What?" Christina shouted.

"I said, 'Are you here to help me mend?'" Mama shouted back.

"I suppose," Christina answered, feeling down and still sad about the move. The wind was howling so loud that it was very hard to hear anybody talk even when they were all shouting or sitting next to each other!

Christina opened Mama's sewing kit and pulled out a needle and thread. Christina then threaded the needle and started to mend one of Stella's dresses.

"Are you all right?" Mama asked after a while.

"Yes, sort of, not really. No, I'm not all right," Christina responded.

"What's the matter?" Mama asked.

"I miss Ruth. I miss school, and I miss our old house," Christina said.

"I miss our old house, too," Mama admitted. "I also miss my parents and my siblings—really all of our family there.

This move has been hard on all of us, even your father."

Suddenly Christina burst into tears. Mama wrapped her arms around Christina for a hug. After a few moments, Christina stopped crying.

"I know what would help," Mama said.

Mama went to the trunk that sat at the end of the bed. She sat down on the ground and opened the trunk. She dug through clothes and other things till she got to the bottom. Then she took out two old, worn books. Christina joined her mother on the floor. Mama handed Christina the books. The first title was *A Midsummer Night's Dream*. The second book was *Hamlet*.

"I loved to read as a child. I still do. I loved reading Shakespeare's books the most," Mama said. "So for my tenth birthday, my parents gave me my two favorite books by Shakespeare. I refused to sell them when we moved here. I want you to have them now."

Christina hugged her mother.

"Thank you! Thank you!" Christina exclaimed. "May I read them now?" Christina let go of her mother.

"Of course," Mother answered. Christina got on the bed and leaned against the wall. She opened the first page of *A Midsummer Night's Dream*.

The snow stopped a few days later. Several days after that, Mama let Christina and her sisters go outside to play.

Christina put on her winter things and opened the front door. She took a few steps outside. The house, the barn, the well, the ground, everything was in snow-bright white. The snow sparkled in the sunlight. There were drifts and piles of snow up against the house the barn, anything with a wall! Suddenly from behind Christina, Stella and Minnie ran by.

"Yahoo!" The two of them jumped into a snow pile.

"Come join us!" Stella called to Christina.

Christina ran and jumped into a pile of snow. Only a few moments after she landed, something cold and hard hit her arm. Christina looked at her arm. She had been hit with a snowball. She looked straight up at Stella, who was grinning. Christina picked up some snow, formed a ball, and then threw it at Stella. It hit her stomach. Then Stella threw a snowball at Christina, and Christina threw a snowball at Minnie. Soon snowballs were flying everywhere.

Papa came out of the barn. He laughed and started to throw snowballs. Everyone was yelling and shouting and laughing. All the noise brought Mama outside.

"What's all the racket?" she asked.

Stella threw a snowball right at Mama! It hit her in the leg. Mama's face turned stern, and then she went inside, closing the door behind her. A few moments later, Mama came back out wearing her winter things. She picked up some snow and threw it at Stella. Stella turned around from where she was throwing snowballs at Minnie. She looked up at Mama, who was smiling.

The whole family was now involved in snowball fight. After a while everyone collapsed on the snow, exhausted and laughing so hard that they all got the hiccups.

Well, Christina thought. *I guess living here isn't so bad. It fact it's fun!*

Roses

Khloe Corrine Marie Beutler

(Age: Fourteen)

Roses remind me of death. Yes, I know it's a morbid thing to say, and yes, I am OK.

People usually see roses as a symbol of romance and purity. I see them as a symbol of death. I cannot stand to see even a single rose without flinching at least slightly.

Roses were the flowers at my grandma's funeral. The bouquet Mom held in her hands as Grandpa reached out to her. All I could do was watch teardrops drip from her cheeks like rain, splattering against the beautiful bouquet. Watch as Grandma lay motionless in the padded coffin, still as beautiful as a rose, as Mom had always said she was.

Roses were the flowers sitting crowded in each vase at Grandpa's funeral as well. At that point I was the only one left to hold Mom, because Dad had also left her by then, leaving me as the only man left in her life.

Roses were the flowers at Mom's funeral…because cars really are death traps, and I should have believed her sooner. I should have trusted that she was right before tragedy happened, before all I had left to remember in my life was a single rose.

I held the white rose in my hand as I walked down the stone steps. Remembering multiple condolences, *I am so sorry for your loss*, I enfolded the flower between my palm and crushed it, dropping it onto the hard concrete.

Life after Mom's death was monotonous. I got up before the sun had fully risen, left early for work, sat alone in my small cubicle, and came home. Sometimes I'd stop for dinner on the way, and that was it.

One day felt different.

I'm not sure how it happened. I'm not sure how I knew from the minute my eyes flew open that the day was going to be special. I just knew. I just had a feeling deep within my bones as sure as I felt happiness or dread or any other emotion humans are capable of feeling. I was sure that day was going to be different.

I decided to walk down the city streets rather than drive. The sun peeked out from beneath clusters of clouds in the sky, shining light into the city. I passed all sorts of shops on my way, almost even stopping to peer through the windows to get a glimpse of what treasures lay beneath their shelves. I felt light and joyful for no reason at all.

I ignored the fact that it was a crisp forty-seven degrees Fahrenheit, that my face was numb and my hands were tingling. I stopped in a small, cozy coffee shop and ordered. A smile suddenly spread across my face. I didn't know why I felt so happy. I didn't know what was wrong with me.

I left the coffee shop feeling refreshed. My feet bounced slightly against the pavement as I walked, and I almost started humming a tune.

As soon as I turned another corner, reality hit. I had no idea where I was. My hands fumbled through my pockets, searching for my cell phone. My heart sank as I realized I had forgotten to take it.

I stopped at the closest shop I could find, a small flower shop. Why a florist? I had no idea, but when I stepped through the doors, my breath was shaky. I could feel my pupils dilate.

The woman was short...not too short but smaller than your typical five-foot-four blonde with blue eyes. Her hair was bright orange.

Tight coils were barely contained in a ponytail of red, curly ribbons. Her lips were baby pink, and freckles danced across her face as she smiled at me.

"Hello! Can I do anything for you?" she asked as I stepped toward the counter. "So what did you do?"

"What?" I stuttered, shifting my weight nervously. "I wasn't...What do you mean?"

"Well, usually when we have guys about your age and your type come in, they are buying flowers to make it up to their *special someone*." She put an emphasis on the last words, her voice sweet.

"No...I...I needed to use the phone." I tried not to sound too nervous. "I don't really have a *special someone*. I'm single. I mean..."

The woman pushed the phone toward me, and I dialed John's number.

I looked up as I talked and found her staring, smiling. She rested her chin against her hand, her elbow against the counter. I hung up.

"What did you mean, *my type*?" I asked curiously.

"I can tell a lot about a person just from looking at him or her." In her eyes, I could see my reflection, and I could almost see my tragic past just from my appearance.

"I'm too late for work. I told John, my boss, I can't come in today."

The woman looked slightly amused, happy, at this announcement.

"One sec," she said, and disappeared into a door with a label printed *Employees only*.

She pushed the door open only moments later. In her hands, she held an object that made my heart sink. A rose.

In that moment I realized that life's too short to dwell over the little things or feel depressed over the big ones. It's too short to not love anyone because you're afraid or to be afraid of love.

Instead of feeling sad when the rose was offered to me, I felt happy, happy for all the moments I did have with loved ones and happy I might possibly have another.

Everything happens for a reason, and I believe I decided to walk to work for a reason. I forgot my phone for a reason.

It amazes me that it took a rose, which to me used to be a symbol of death, to change my perspective and outlook.

What used to symbolize death to me in that moment began to symbolize life—the lives of those I loved. In that moment I felt that life and love were possible again.

"I'm off work at five," she said.

The woman, Marley, as her name tag read, smiled shyly. "Do you want to do something?"

So instead of my feeling depressed at the sight of the rose, my hand reached out and grabbed it, a smile on my cheeks.

A Window to Young Minds

Dream

Sivaranjani Velmurugan

(Age: Eleven)

*F*ive-year-old Nick lay in his bed and listened to the gentle sound of the clock ticking in his bedroom. Tick, tock. Nick glanced at the clock, and it showed that it was exactly midnight.

Nick stared at the full moon as its silver light illuminated his room. Click, bam! Alarmed, Nick sat straight on his bed. Slowly he peered under his bed. He couldn't believe his eyes!

There was a trap door right there!

How come he had never seen this before? As he crawled under the bed for a closer look, he discovered a slide. Nick carefully placed one foot in the slide and then the other, and before he knew it, he was sliding down, down, down, on an amazing adventure! Nick's heart started beating faster as he got closer and closer to a source of light. Thump, thump. Swoosh! The ride ended.

Nick stepped on the grass, which was as soft as cotton candy. He could not believe his eyes. He rubbed his eyes and blinked. He was still able to see it.

"Whoa!" he cried.

There right before his eyes were toys! Not just any old toys but toys that were moving and talking. The toys and dolls were unmistakably alive!

"Hi! Hello? Who are you?"

Nick turned around to see a wooden duck talking to him.

"I'm Nick!" he replied.

"I'm Debby the Webby Feet!" quacked the duck.

"Whoa! What kind of toy are you?"

Nick whirled around and saw a giant teddy bear about three times as large as he was who was examining him in shock.

"I'm a person, not a toy!" Nick told him.

"A what?" asked the bear.

"A person!" repeated Nick.

"I'm Ted the Teddy Bear!" growled the bear.

"I've never heard of a person before, but you are welcome to join us in the feast!" cried the bear, and before Nick knew it, he was dragged into a garden and seated at a table with a bowlful of carrots before him. He groaned. He hated carrots. But he didn't want to disappoint the toys.

I wish that these were Cheetos! thought Nick as he hesitated to eat. There was a sudden cracking sound, and when Nick peered into the bowl for carrots, there were Cheetos instead. His eyes shone with glory and wonder as he reached for one.

"Hold on a second!" squeaked a mouse. "How did that happen?"

All the others murmured in wonder.

"I don't know how it happened, but all I did was wish for chips!" Nick replied.

"Then your wish came true!" roared a stuffed-animal lion. "Oh, by the way, I'm Lammy the Lion! Nice to meet you, person!" Lammy grunted as he introduced himself.

"And I'm Mike the Mouse!" squeaked the mouse who had spoken earlier.

"Nice to meet you all!" Nick hollered as he looked over at

A Window to Young Minds

the toys who had gathered here for the feast.

"Wait!" cried Penny the Pig. "If you did magic once, then you can do it again!"

The crowd murmured in agreement. Nick carefully scanned a bowl of oranges.

"This isn't serious!" he told himself. "Take it easy!"

The crowd whispered to each other, and some toys squeezed their way to the front for a better view of the mysterious magician. Nick squeezed his eyes shut and concentrated on one thought.

I wish that these oranges were Doritos! he thought as he pictured an image Doritos in his head. When he opened his eyes, a packet of Doritos had replaced the bowl of oranges. Everyone was talking at once.

"Wow!" squeaked Mike.

"Magic!" growled Ted.

"Mind power!" squealed Penny the Pig.

Nick ignored the noise.

"This isn't real!" he told himself.

Instantly he noticed an owl made of different colored and designed fabrics soaring toward them, but it was gliding directly under a falling apple tree. Everyone's attention was drawn to Nick's actions, so no one except Nick noticed this. Nick had to do something fast before it was too late. Nick raced toward the tree, and with all his might, he stood under the weight of the tree for a moment. Then he managed to push it back up to its vertical position. When he finally turned back to the owl, everyone was gasping at him.

"You have superspeed!" roared Lammy.

"You have superstrength!" oinked Penny.

"Hey! Why are you so late for the feast?" Mike asked the

owl. "Look whom we met!" he squeaked excitedly as he nudged Nick.

"Oh! I know all about you!" the owl hooted as he glanced at Nick.

"My name is Waldo the Wise Owl. I spent some time back in my tree house to solve the mystery of how you arrived here. I didn't miss anything that happened while I wasn't here, because I watched everything from my tree house, which is very high in a tree. According to my calculations and proof, every full moon a trapdoor located under your bed is unlocked when the moon's light shines on it. This allows you to enter our magical world. Your magical powers make you a superhero, and they must be used for a good cause," Waldo finished.

After a delicious feast, Nick stood before the trapdoor that he had first came through. It was time to say good-bye. He waved to his new friends.

"I'll see you all next full moon!" he said, and with that, he opened the trap door and stepped into the elevator inside and watched the image of his friends fade away from sight as he accelerated upward. When the elevator stopped, he opened the trapdoor and climbed out of the trapdoor. Then he locked the trapdoor and watched it disappear. Nick was just an ordinary boy in his world, but he was a superhero in Toy World.

Daylight was streaming into the room. Nick sat up in bed and looked around and wondered about what he had just seen and had done. Trying to figure out if his adventure had been real, he crawled under the bed and squinted at the floor and strained his eyes to find a trapdoor. He could only see the plain, flat, wooden floor, so he crawled out.

"Nick!" his mother yelled. "Only twenty more minutes

before school starts!"

"Mom, I just had the most amazing dream ever! So first—" Nick started before his mother flew into the room.

She was wearing her jacket backwards, holding her hairbrush in one hand, and clutching her cup of coffee in the other.

"Not now, sweetie. Hurry up, or you'll be late for school and I'll be late for work!" she panicked as she cut him short before he could describe his dream. Nick understood that this was *not* the time to talk to his mom, so he tried telling his dad in the car while he was driving him to school.

"Dad, I had this really cool dream," he started, but his dad wasn't in right mood.

"There's no time now, Nick. If you don't get to school fast, you'll be late and I'll be late for work!" his dad almost yelled.

So Nick trudged into his classroom with hanging head and drooping shoulders. Suddenly he had an idea. Nick could recite his story to his teacher at school.

"Ms. Green, I had this magnificent dream about talking toys," he started, but his teacher began to shriek.

"Nick, I can't listen to your story now, and this test is timed. So will you please take your test!"

Nick thought that maybe his friends would want to hear his story at recess.

"Guys, want to hear my super dream about me as a hero?" he asked, but they weren't at all interested.

"Dude, let's play tag instead," they advised.

So Nick's last hope was the lady at his after-school program, Ms. Smith.

"Ms. Smith, do you have time hear my story?" he

questioned politely.

"I'm afraid I don't," she answered as she helped others with their homework.

Tears flowed down his face as Nick sat on a bench, all by himself, ever so lonely.

Is the world really too busy to listen to my dream? he thought helplessly.

That night Nick lined up all his stuffed animals that he had on his bed—Debby the Duck, Ted the Teddy Bear, Lammy the Lion, Mike the Mouse, Penny the Pig, and Waldo the Owl—and started narrating his story. He included every detail he could remember, and they all sat quietly and listened to everything he told them, which gave him a sense of happiness.

He wondered if he could go back to Toy Town in his dream the next full moon to be a superhero again.

A feeling of comfort fell over him as he fell asleep, and all his worries vanished.

A Window to Young Minds

Thirteenth Tunnel Street

Elliot Hui

(Age: Twelve)

*W*hen I discovered what the party was really about and who was there, I was completely terrified!

It all began on that Halloween night. When I burst into my room after an exhausting day at school, a wave of fresh air hit me like a gust of wind. Now I was ready for trick-or-treating.

I went to my dresser to grab my new costume. The costume was a homemade zombie pirate. It was a pain to make, but it was worth it in the end. When my hand was less than an inch away from the drawer's handle, I noticed a strong, musty smell filling the bedroom. I scanned the room until my eyes fell upon a crumpled note smeared in mud pinned on my costume! As I carefully unfolded the note, I touched the fresh mud, which had pieces of dry leaves on it.

The mysterious note was scrawled in red ink and eerily stated,

> *Dan,*
>
> *Come to the Mansion of Darkness on Thirteenth Tunnel Street for a party.*
>
> *From,*
>
> *Dracula*

I thought excitedly, *Fantastic! My first invitation to an eerie*

Halloween party! I tossed the note away and donned my costume.

My mother, who works as a police officer, called, "Dan! You have until eight o'clock to go trick-or-treating!"

I nodded to her, and then I hopped on my bike and raced toward the mansion with pulsing curiosity and excitement inside my head.

As I arrived, my watch read 6:55 p.m., which meant I had about one hour left. I heaved the gigantic door knocker a few times, which created echoing thuds.

Suddenly a realistic-looking vampire popped his head around the rustic door and said, "Ah, yes! You must be Dan, the pirate zombie. Come in. Come in."

He then gestured for me to come in by opening the door wider. I walked in and asked the host, "Where did you get that realistic costume?"

"What…what do you mean?" Dracula stammered.

But before I could think of an answer, I saw all the partygoers.

There were mummies, zombies, aliens, and any other kind of creatures you could think of. However, the majority of them was huddling around a blindfolded, ferocious werewolf trying to pin a tail with a needle on Frankenstein!

Confused, I stood there and watched as the werewolf eventually cornered and pounced on Frankenstein, sending them both tumbling to the ground.

As the werewolf raised the needle high above his head, poised to attack, the bystanders chanted, "Pin the tail! Pin the tail!"

He was about to stick the pin on Frankenstein but not before I ceased the outrageous mayhem.

"Stop! You are going to hurt him!" I pleaded.

Everyone turned around and stared at me as if I were insane, but dead silence swept over them. I rushed toward the werewolf and repeated, "You may seriously injure the poor kid with the razor-sharp needle."

Frankenstein stood up and revealed himself to be over eleven feet tall! As he loomed over me, he scoffed and then roared, "I am no weak human. *I am Frankenstein!*"

Shocked, I took several steps backward, stumbled into the door, and questioned, "You mean that is not a mask you are wearing, and this is not a costume party?"

I was trying to buy myself some time to escape.

"Dan is an imposter! Bring him to me!" commanded Dracula in a menacing tone and raising a long, slender finger at me. With a low growl, the monsters dashed toward me with surprising speed, but I was already out the door. I ran to my bike and pedaled with lightning speed back home, down the shadowed streets.

The monsters roared in determination, chased me for a couple of blocks, and then fell behind in my dust! I sighed in relief and slowed down my pace to conserve my energy. Suddenly the monsters flanked ahead of me, popping out of nearby bushes, trash cans, behind houses, trees, and almost any other hiding spot you could think of, coming toward me like a wave!

I dodged the first few, swerving my bike with all my strength to avoid them. Then a cluster of them appeared in front of me through the obscure fog, like magic, and I could see my house just less than a few yards away! The pack of monsters was less than a few feet away, and I swung my legs off my bike so that I could flee on foot.

Only then I realized my vital mistake. There was a speed bump in front of me! Everything happened in slow motion. The bike rotated forward; my hands' knuckles were white from tightly gripping the handle bars. I thought I would not survive the bone-crushing fall on to the pavement and, more importantly, the monsters behind me. Luckily the centrifugal force flung me away. My body soared through the air, and I miraculously landed safely on the plush doormat of our house!

The door to my house was left open, so I scrambled into the house. Glancing back at the enraged monsters, I saw their drained determination. I slammed the door closed and threw on the dead bolt. The atmosphere was suddenly calm once again.

Knowing that they would be caught by the police if they broke in, the monsters trudged back to the mansion in defeat. The pins in the lock quietly rattled after I shut the door.

As I walked back to my room drenched in sweat, I wore a weary grin of victory. My mother was inside waiting for me, her hands on her hips.

"Daniel Martin Reed! You went trick-or-treating? Where is your candy?" she inquired.

Then she harshly scolded, "It is one in the morning, Daniel! You are twelve years old, and you should be more responsible!"

My head lowered to my watch. It read 12:55 a.m., nearly five hours late. I knew that she would not understand my extraordinary experience, the mansion, monsters, plus the chase, so I breathlessly replied, "I was at a costume party, and I got a whole lot more than I bargained for."

I am Brisby

Fisher Lynn Mishmash

(Age: Twelve)

I am Brisby.

I have been wandering for a year or two. I don't know; I am just a dog.

There is not much to eat, for it's almost winter. I have grown thin over the last few years, and you can see my ribs. Right now I am by a lake. The water is cold, and ice is starting to form. I hope I will make it through the cold Alaskan winter. I have been hoping for a while; I am thin, and I am not sure I will make it. I wish I was home—near the warmth, my family.

But now...

There is only wilderness. Sometimes I want to give up and let the bears eat me, but I push on; it's harder than you think. Trust me.

It all began on a warm June day.

My family was on a camping trip. I remember it well. It was warm and sunny; the flowers were in bloom, and there were all sorts of good smells. We were having fun, and I was learning a new trick. Then out of nowhere, we heard a growl. Following the growl came a big, black bear! Someone screamed! I don't know who it was, because the bear had grabbed me in his teeth. I yelped! The bear growled, picked me up, and carried me of into the woods. I bit the bear, and he dropped me. I ran and didn't stop.

By the time I got over my scare, I was about two or three miles from our campsite. It was dark; I could not see much. I found an old pine tree and curled up under it. That night I dreamt about my family and thought I had to go back.

I woke up early and started the long walk back to our campsite. By the time I reached it, there was nobody in sight. I waited. And waited some more. No one.

I barked, a rare thing for me to do, but no one came. I was very hungry by now, so I looked for food. All I found was a bit of soggy hot-dog bun with a little mustard on it. It did not look or smell appetizing, but I ate it anyway; I was starved. I scavenged some more food, an old carrot, some wild blueberries, and a little cracker. Humans are messy.

By the time I had found enough food to keep my belly from growling, it had started to rain, and I was getting soaked. I needed to find shelter quickly! I looked around. Nothing to hide under! I was getting desperate when I saw it. A small creek had eroded a cave in the bank. I ran. Lightning flashed. I jumped the creek. A tree fell in front of me. The rain poured down. I reached the cave. I was safe from the rain and lightning. I was tired and soon fell asleep to the sound of the rain.

When I woke, I was cold and wet. I looked out of the cave and saw that the creek was not a creek; it was a river! It had almost risen to the entrance of the cave.

The rain continued to pour down. I saw a wall of water rushing toward me. Before I could react, it hit me. The cave collapsed, and I was swept off my feet. The icy water pushed me down, I pawed at it, but I could not get to the surface. Was this the end?

I closed my eyes and waited.

With a thud, I hit something. I opened my eyes and saw that I was on a gravel bar. I took a big breath of air and coughed up some water. I was safe. Or so I thought.

I looked around. To my left, there was nothing but water—fast, cold, dangerous water. To my right, there was a massive pile of sticks and more water. I was trapped on an island, a bare island with nothing but a pile of sticks.

I considered swimming but decided against it. I was faced with another problem. The water was getting higher and my island smaller. I couldn't do anything but wait.

After a day of rain, it finally stopped. The water slowly retreated far enough for me to get to safety. After so long without food, I was starving.

I began to hunt for food. The river had carried me far from any civilization, so there was no human food to be found. I sniffed the air and smelled food, not human food but food. I followed the smell. It got stronger, and before I knew it, I had found the source of the smell. It seemed to be a cache from some animal.

I dug in the soft dirt and found some meat. It was a little old, but I was starving. I began to eat; then out of nowhere, a gray blur shot out and nipped me. It was a wolf pup. He licked my face and whined. He looked hungry, too, so I shared my food. After he had his fill, I ate the rest.

The wolf pup howled, and a louder, deeper howl returned. A larger, bigger wolf appeared, and behind it was a whole wolf pack! They growled but saw the wolf pup playing joyfully.

A big gray wolf with a black tail stepped forward, her ears back, a submissive sign. She sniffed me and then licked me. She seemed to be inviting me into the pack. She then grabbed the wolf pup by his scruff and walked back into the woods. I followed cautiously.

It has been two days since I joined the wolf pack, and I am well fed. The alpha female taught me how to hunt with the pack.

In the morning, we hunt. We sleep in the afternoon, and then we hunt again; when we are done eating, we play. When it is time to sleep again, I go to my den. My den is under a rock and has plenty of room for me to move. It is quite cozy and smells of pine. I continue this routine with the wolves for many months.

It is September now, and we are fattening up for winter. We are hunting for food a lot more. Silently we are stalking a rabbit, when a loud bang stops us in our tracks. The rabbit runs. Then another loud bang. And then silence. The big gray wolf is on the ground—with a fatal wound on her shoulder. She was bleeding a lot, and with one last breath her life ended. We have just lost a great leader. Now that there is no one to lead us, we scatter. We probably will not make it to summer.

It had been a few days since we had eaten. Some of the weaker wolves had already gone. I was forced to leave my den and look for food. I wandered away from the pack, never to return. I hunted, but nothing stirred. I wandered farther and farther.

Finally I spotted a lake. On the lake, I saw a bird, a duck, who must have missed the migration. I ran toward the duck. There was ice on the lake, I jumped on to it and kept running. The duck spotted me and started to pump his wings. I ran faster. I was almost upon the duck when a crack appeared in the ice, and I went down.

I hit the bottom with a thud. I pawed at the water and went up a little, but I just sank back down. I pawed again, and this time I rose. I hit the ice and with a crack broke through. I tried to climb up on the ice, but it kept breaking.

Finally after smashing through quite a bit of ice, I found a spot thick enough to climb on. Cautiously I inched my way back to shore. I shook the icy water from my fur and looked for shelter. All I found was a bare willow tree. It was not much shelter, but it was better than none.

When I woke up, it was even colder. And there was no food anywhere. I walked and found nothing. Too tired to go on, I lay down.

I must then have fallen asleep, for when I woke up, the sun was setting and I was freezing. I barely had enough energy to walk back to my tree. When I got there, I curled up and went to sleep. That night snow fell and wind blew. I became buried in snow, but I did not care; it kept me warm. I stayed like this for many days until hunger forced me out. When I emerged, it was clear and sunny. I looked for food and saw a bird. I ran, using the last of my energy. I leaped. This was it. If I caught it, I would live. If I did not...

I flew through the air.

About Lune Spark Books

Lune Spark Books aims to encourage children to engage in creating writing. We work with parents and young writers to promote creative fiction writing to help identify talent. We run annual competitions and creative writing classes and publish short stories from the young writers. For more details, visit us at http://lunespark.com/youngwriters/.

For the details of the contest or enroll in the contest, please visit us at http://lunespark.com/youngwriters/storycontest/.

Follow us on social media to keep up with the latest updates. https://www.facebook.com/youngwriterscontest/. https://twitter.com/LuneSparkLLC.

Other Books by Lune Spark

1. My Teacher Hilda
(Children's picture book series)

Playing is an important part of children's learning and development. Appropriate for the children in the age ranges three years to

eight years, this book series focuses on play-based early learning. The cute animal characters continuously engage in fun-filled learning activities. This series also aims to help kids learn socialization before they join kindergarten to help make this important transition easier.

2. Surviving Gretchen
(Children, family, friendship)

Thick as thieves since birth, Abby and Emma aren't just best friends. They're like two life forces sharing the same soul, certain that the ties that bind them can weather any storm. Then a pretentious prima donna of a girl named Gretchen blows into their lives, swirling across the landscape of their friendship like a hurricane. Will Abby and Emma survive Gretchen?

3. Coinman: An Untold Conspiracy
(Literary fiction, humor, satire, office parody)

A clerk called Coinman can't stop jingling the coins in his pocket. It's a simple addiction, but it's one that comes to rule his life.